I0683284

Compelled To Kill

A Bob Ryan Mystery

John Buchak

Copyright 2014 by John Buchak

All rights reserved. No part of this publication may be reproduced or transmitted in any form or by any means, electronic or mechanical, including photocopy, recording or any information storage and retrieval system, without permission in writing from the copyright owner.

Printed in the United States of America

ISBN: 9780692265093

For the reason of any type of litigation, the following statement has been included in this novel. This novel is a work of fiction. Names, characters, places and incidents either are the product of the author's imagination or are used fictitiously. Any resemblance to actual persons, living or dead, events, or locales is entirely coincidental.

Cover Design: Karin Buchak

Photos by www.dreamstime.com

Acknowledgments

First off, I want to thank all the members of my family for the support they have given me ever since I first started writing my first novel.

Next, I need to thank the members of IWOSC/ Independent Writers of Southern California, of which I am very proud to be a member.

My thanks must also go out to two friends, Sylvia Cary and Rick Rofman, who helped me get this book ready for publication.

I thank my daughter Karin, who has always been a blessing to me and enjoys working with printed words and images, for all her help and support.

1

Ralph Creto slowly and quietly got out of bed, carefully trying not to wake his wife of sixteen years. As he turned on the bathroom light, he heard her say, "Honey, it's ok, I'm awake, I'll make coffee and get your lunch ready for you while you take your shower."

Ralph, a handsome burly-looking guy of thirty-eight, loved his job as a computer technician, but always being the tall guy in whatever group he was standing in, loved his basketball games on the weekends with his buddies.

At the start of his junior year in high school, Ralph was a modest and fairly tall 6'1," but sprouted up to a towering 6'7" by the next summer break.

Esther attended all of Ralph's high school games and soon started dating him when they met after a friend introduced them.

Always a man of honesty and integrity, he would have stood tall even if he been five foot two, and Esther saw the quality of the young man she had just started dating.

Here it was many years later and other than the weekend games with his friends, Ralph devoted the majority of his time to his wonderful wife.

It was a day like any other with Ralph getting ready to leave for work at 7:30a.m., then waiting for the 7:45a.m.bus that stopped at the corner.

Just before walking out the door, Ralph kissed his wife on the cheek and told her he would see her around 6p.m., and maybe they could catch a movie that night after work.

Stepping out of the front door Ralph paused, looked up at the sky, whispered softly, "What a wonderful day," took a deep breath of the cool morning air, and collapsed, falling down the twelve cement steps to the sidewalk below!

A neighbor across the street who happened to be looking out the front window of her apartment watched in horror, as Ralph was not moving.

Calling first her neighbor Esther, a good friend for many years, the woman then called 911 and reported what she had witnessed.

When the paramedics arrived, a quick examination revealed that Ralph was dead from a bullet wound just above his right temple, before he stopped rolling down the steps.

Esther's neighbor Judith knocked on her door and told her what had happened. While Ester stood at the top of the steps crying hysterically, Judith tried to comfort her.

As neighbors and passersby started to move in for a closer look, the paramedics had to ask everyone, "Please step back, and do not contaminate the crime scene."

Screaming at the top of her lungs, Ester said, "What do you mean crime scene?"

The paramedics looked at each other and then one of them answered, "Your husband has been shot, ma'am."

"Shot? What do you mean shot? You must be mistaken. He was on his way to work. Who would shoot him?"

The older of the two paramedics responded, "Ma'am, I don't know who or why, but we're not mistaken, he has been shot and the police are on the way."

As Esther sat down on the top step of the porch, the paramedics sealed off the area with yellow tape with the words, "CRIME SCENE DO NOT CROSS."

With a blanket covering her husband at the foot of the steps, each time Ester looked down at her husband's uncovered legs, and one missing shoe, she would cry uncontrollably.

Approximately fifteen minutes had passed by when the first of several police cars pulled up in front of the building and blocked the street.

By this time, the entire building had come out to see what had happened in their normally quiet neighborhood.

With the arrival of two detectives from Homicide Division, and an inspector from Crime Scene Investigation, the neighbors in the surrounding buildings seemed to pour into the street, all asking questions no one had answers for yet.

Many of the blue-jacketed police officers had already started searching the area and asking questions, trying to fill in some of the blanks, but no one would come forward with any information.

Other then the neighbor from across the street, no one admitted seeing or hearing anything.

After a brief conversation with the paramedics, Detective Joseph Lucas walked up the steps of the brownstone building and sat down next to Esther.

Introducing himself and offering his sincere condolences, he asked her if there was anything she might know that could offer any kind of explanation for the shooting of her husband.

Through her tears and broken speech, she told him, "I have no idea what this is all about. My husband has been a good man, and a good father." Then a look of fear came over her face and she said, "My God. What am I going to tell our daughter?"

The detective stood up, offering his hand to the grieving widow and asking, "Mrs. Creto, would you feel more comfortable talking in your apartment?"

"Detective, I don't think I'll ever feel comfortable again, but thank you for your concern."

Esther's neighbor Judith held her hand as they walked back into the house, and when they all sat at the kitchen table, she told Esther, "I'm here for you dear. Whatever you need, just call me."

Through his questioning, the detective found that Ester and her husband had moved to Queens, New York sixteen years earlier, right after they were married in Los Angeles, California.

Though Ralph was born in New York, his parents had moved to California when he was only a child, his dream always being to return to his birthplace.

After his parents died in a tragic house fire when he was just a young man of twenty, he decided that the time was right for the move to start a new life in his hometown.

It was not to be at that time, because of a chance meeting arranged by a friend, with a soft-spoken beautiful woman named Esther.

Esther, a California native, had lost her mom to cancer only a couple of years earlier, and her dad had remarried and moved to Canada.

It was love at first sight for the two lonely people, and they started dating from that day on, until their marriage two years later.

Writing down names of Ralph's employer, close friends, local hangouts, and any other information the detective thought might help in the investigation, he once again said, "I'm so sorry for your loss, Mrs. Creto. I will do all I can to find the people responsible for your husband's murder."

As members of the Coroner's Department bagged up her husband's body, Ester watched through her front window crying and asking God, "Why, why did you take him from me?"

Information gathered by officers questioning neighbors, yielded one clue, that a gray four door Mercedes had been parked just down the street before all the excitement started, but now it was gone.

2

Barbara Beth Jones operated a flower store she had suddenly and unexpectedly inherited when her father passed away six years earlier. The store was located on Springfield Avenue in the small east coast town of Irvington, New Jersey. Although she had sworn never to move back to New Jersey after moving away a long twenty-two years ago, taking control of the store and helping with the care of her aging mother was the choice she felt she had to make.

Barbara's beloved grandmother had passed away at an early age when Barbara was just a teenager, and her mother was never the same after this death.

Leaving her home in Los Angeles, was a hard decision to make, but it was the right thing to do in her mind, always as she was a person who never ran away from responsibility.

On a cold and wet April morning, starting the day the way she had for the past few years, Barbara stopped at her local donut shop to purchase her large coffee and buttermilk donut, then spent a few minutes with her friend Ruth who was the proprietor and next-door neighbor of the flower shop.

Her dear friend Ruth would constantly remind her, "You know sweetheart those donuts, no matter how good they taste, are big factor in your oversized caboose."

With a smile on her face, and a cute little wink, Barbara would remind Ruth, "Don't forget, dear, to tie your tiny little butt to something heavy if a strong wind starts to blow."

After a hardy laugh they wished each other a very happy and productive day. Then Barbara pulled up her collar, buttoned her jacket, and left the donut shop for the short walk next door.

While fumbling with her keys in the rain, at the front door to the flower shop, Barbara suddenly fell to the ground, dropping her coffee, donut, and purse.

Ten minutes had passed by before Barbara was discovered lying on the sidewalk, but it didn't matter; she was dead before her body touched the ground. When the paramedics arrived, they confirmed that she died from a single bullet wound to the head.

When the Irvington Police Department and Homicide Detectives arrived at the scene, everything was handled in a very professional manner, with the area being sealed off and prospective witnesses being questioned.

There seemed to be no rhyme or reason to Barbara's shooting and after six months of investigation, her murder went on the books as an unsolved crime, not a closed case, but just put on the back burners as the caseload of the police department increased.

3

Returning home in his beat up twenty-year old Ford station wagon after a pleasant day of fishing off his favorite pier in Sarasota, Florida, retired LAPD Detective Francis Robert Ryan had just walked in his apartment when the phone started ringing.

At first, Ryan was so pleased to hear the caller's voice on the other end of the line, but that soon changed.

The caller was Dorothy Metzger, the wife of Ryan's old partner in Los Angeles, California. Almost everyone who knew Ryan other than close friends used only his last name. Leo Metzger and Ryan were partners on the LAPD for twelve years, before Ryan decided he had had enough, and retired to Sarasota.

The two of them hadn't spoken to each other in over three years since Ryan's retirement to Florida except to wish Dorothy and Leo a happy twenty-fifth wedding anniversary.

As Dorothy tried to contain herself it was obvious to Ryan that something was terribly wrong, and that this call was not for a casual conversation.

Through the tears, Dorothy said, "He's dead Robert, Leo's dead. They said he committed suicide, but he would never do that, someone killed him."

"Dorothy, take a deep breath and tell me what happened."

"Leo and his partner, Danny Polito, were working on an investigation involving a bookkeeper in Reseda, and they were keeping her under constant surveillance.

Leo watched her each morning, and Danny in the afternoon, with two other detectives watching her every move through the evening hours."

I don't know what the case was about, and as you know, Leo never liked to talk about any of his cases, but he said he was upset at what he was seeing."

Ryan asked her how Leo had died, and Dorothy broke down and started crying again.

Taking a few seconds to regain her composure, Dorothy said, "They said he put his service revolver to his head and pulled the trigger, and he died instantly.

"It's not true, Robert. It's not true, he would never kill himself. Please, Robert you have to find out what happened; no one will believe me."

Trying to reassure her that he would check into what was going on, and that he would be there just as soon as he could get a plane reservation, he asked, "When did it happen, and have they released Leo's body to the mortuary yet?"

She told him that the Coroner's office has not released Leo yet, and they were sure the bullet was self-inflicted.

Telling her that he would make a few phone calls, he then asked, "Sweetheart, is Captain Hodges still in charge of the department?"

"No, he retired last year, and Bill Robinson replaced him. You remember him, don't you, Robert?"

"Yes dear, the name sounds very familiar. Give me a few minutes to place him in my aging mind."

"Bill relocated from Ventura a year ago, Robert, with his wife, after his youngest son graduated from college and moved away."

Remembering Bill from a case they worked on many years ago, Ryan said, "You mean that big red-faced Englishman with the soft spoken voice?"

"Yes, that's him. He took over when Jim Hodges retired, and made a lot of changes in the department."

Ryan told Dorothy he would call her back after he spoke to Captain Robinson, and then would let her know when he would be arriving in Los Angeles.

Before hanging up the phone, he told her, "Dot, I know Leo would never do this to himself, and I promise you I will find out who's responsible."

Bob Ryan and Leo Metzger were two of the most un-likely partners the police department could ever put together. Ryan in his early days was a hard drinking, foul mouthed, hard ass of a cop, but honest to the point that no one would believe. He suffered from high blood pressure, hair loss, over weight, bad teeth, a severe drinking problem, and flat feet.

Leo on the other hand was a happily married man, college educated, church going, health conscience, a stickler on appearance, and a respectable member of the community, who happened to be a servant of the people, in the Los Angeles Police Department.

Leo always saw the glass as half full, and that there was always some good in everyone.

Ryan, on the other hand, saw it as half empty, and started looking for another beer to fill it up.

Ryan looked like he bought his clothes outside of the Goodwill stores, you know, the stuff they throw out for the trash collector, those great duds that never made it to the For Sale rack.

Leo always looked like he belonged on the cover of GQ Magazine, with never a hair out of place or a wrinkle in his clothes.

A very unlikely match-up, but they worked together like common sense and wisdom, although sometimes Ryan used a little more brute force and less sense.

As Ryan sat in his soft cushy chair after his conversation with Dorothy, his mind drifted back to better times with his good friend Leo, and swore to himself that he would find the truth about his death.

4

Driving around Los Angeles over the past twenty-five years has been a pleasure Otis Reyas has enjoyed since joining the other Cabbies at the Yellow Cab Company.

He first applied for the job after obtaining his citizenship in the US after many years of low paying, demeaning employment under some of the worst possible conditions.

Otis, born in Panama, spoke of the day he was sworn in as a citizen many times, expressing pride as he pointed to a US flag pin he wore on his Cabbie hat. Meeting and marrying Francis Tobias and his love for her was his main reason for living, or so he told everyone who would listen.

Otis, a tall slender man, approximately 6'4", and weighing around 165 pounds, was sometimes called Stretch, by his fellow workers, and was thought of as a kind and gentle sole by all who knew him.

Francis, a sweet and soft-spoken little woman, who stood just over five foot, and weighed about ten pounds more then her husband, was like a beautiful model in Otis's eyes.

For years the couple tried without success to have a family, but it appeared that it was not meant to be for the loving couple.

Francis would meet Otis each night as his shift ended, and the two of them would walk the five city blocks to their home, sometimes stopping along the way to have a bite to eat at their favorite restaurant, 'The Smooth Shell,' a seafood and steak establishment owned by another Panamanian they had met years earlier.

Like clockwork, at 8pm six nights a week, without fail Francis was there.

Then one Tuesday night in May, as Otis waited outside of the Cab Barn, he paced anxiously for twenty minutes, before going back in to the building to use the phone to call his dear Francis.

Letting the phone ring ten times before hanging up, he then walked swiftly to his home fearing that something was wrong.

Finding the front door to the apartment building unlocked and partially opened, Otis climbed the stairs two at a time until he reached the second floor.

With his keys in his hand he unlocked the apartment door and quickly entered.

The two-bedroom apartment was laid out in a railroad car layout, with the living room being first in line, followed by the kitchen, then the two bedrooms.

Calling her name Otis heard no response, as he went through each room opening doors that were never closed before, he realized something was wrong.

Opening the door to the front bedroom he screamed in horror, as he saw his beloved wife lying on the bed with a nylon stocking over her head, and a rope tied tightly around her neck.

Running to her side, not thinking about disturbing evidence, he untied the rope and removed the stocking then began trying to revive her, but it was too late, she was dead.

The downstairs neighbor, hearing the screams from Otis came upstairs, and when told what had happened, called 911 and told them a murder had been committed.

With the arrival of the LAPD, a crime scene investigation team also showed up, and Otis was questioned extensively, and reprimanded for removing the stocking and the rope from his wife's body.

Rising from his chair, Otis made a grab for the officer who dared to suggest that he should not have tried to revive his wife and disturb clues.

Without knowing the relationship between Otis and Francis, and how strong their love for each other was, the police first assumed and suspected Otis as the killer.

After questioning fellow workers of his, who gave him an ironclad alibi, it was obvious to the detectives that Otis could not be the murderer.

The Coroner confirmed that Francis had been dead approximately two hours, before being discovered, and there had not been any sexual invasion of her body.

With the apartment being examined for fingerprints, other then Francis or Otis, nothing was found to give the police any leads in the case.

Once again a murder had been committed with no reason or connection to any other crime, and went on the books as unsolved.

5

Ryan sat at his desk staring at the hanging light from the ceiling, with his mind drifting back to his days on the LAPD, remembering his old friend Leo.

The old crusty veteran had to reach for the Kleenex box on the bookcase next to his desk, as several tears dripped down his unshaven cheeks.

Wanting to just pack a bag and get on the first flight to Los Angeles, Ryan knew he had to leave the crime solving to the younger officers and hope that they would keep in touch with him as the investigation of Leo's suicide was handled in the proper way.

Opening his address book to double check for the phone number of his old police precinct, Ryan looked and said out loud, "Of course that's the number!" But the problem was, he didn't remember.

The number he was looking up, was a number he had called thousands of times during his twenty-eight years with the LAPD, and now his memory was just not as sharp as it used to be.

Making the call and being put on hold several times, as he asked to speak with Capt. Bill Robinson., Ryan started to get frustrated.

So when the forth person asked him who he was waiting to talk with, Ryan said, "This is Detective Robert Ryan in Sarasota Florida, and I've been waiting to talk with Capt. Robinson for twenty minutes, and if one more person asks me who I want to talk with, I will personally come out there and kick his ass, now please put me through to the Captain."

The next voice Ryan heard was, "Hello, this is Capt. Robinson, how can I help you?"

When the captain heard the raspy voice and the name, he remembered him well and asked, "So what do I owe this honor to Ryan?"

Ryan explained how Dorothy Metzger had called and informed him of Leo's death, and was told that Leo had committed suicide.

The Captain said, "We haven't completed our investigation yet Ryan, we're still checking out all the evidence, but it looks like Leo just decided he couldn't take it anymore and ended his life."

"Captain, I worked beside Leo Metzger for twelve years, and outside of his wife, no one knew him better then me, and I'm telling you there is no way in hell that man would commit suicide."

"Ryan, you've been away from the job for a long time now, what's it been, four or five years, things change, people change, stress takes over and people do the unexpected."

"Captain, can I at least get a copy of the investigation report, so I can look at it and then I can talk with Leo's widow and assure her that everything that can be done is being done?"

"Ryan you know that the reports are confidential, I can't turn that over to just anyone."

Hearing that outraged Ryan, and he responded, "Just anyone, Bill, I remember when you needed my help when you were still in Ventura. I didn't think twice to helping
you out, when you were a snot-nosed rookie who could just about wipe his own ass years ago."

"That's uncalled for Ryan, you of all people know those reports are confidential."

"Yes I do, and I also know that Leo would never commit suicide, please Bill, I know it's a big favor to ask, but please this is one of our own."

The Captain paused a little and said, "Ryan, if you were closer by, I might be able to do something, but your way the hell on the other side of the country."

"Not for long Captain, I'll be in LA tomorrow night to try to comfort Leo's widow."

The Captain told him, "Come in and see me, and try not to let anyone know the reason for your visit, other then saying a quick hello to old friends, and I'll put together a package for you."

"Thank you Bill, I won't forget this."

"That's just it Ryan, you will forget this, because it never happened, and I have no idea where you obtained your information."

6

Helen Fisher was enjoying a Sunday afternoon visit with her daughter and grandchildren in Bakersfield, California when an unexpected rain shower hit, lasting about an hour.

Helen's daughter Joan, son in law John, grandchildren Cindy and Tyler, had moved to Bakersfield three years earlier when John's employer relocated his business to improve sales.

Living about a hundred miles south in Los Angeles, where she has lived for forty-five years, Helen makes the trip once a month to visit the only family she has left since her husband passed away.

Being seventy-six and in good physical and mental condition, Helen loves to spend her free time driving to visit old friends who can no longer get around themselves.

For the past eleven years, since her retirement from working for the city, Helen has volunteered her services for many causes, including children's services, Meals on wheels, Salvation Army, clothing drives, and any other organization to help the community.

While enjoying her day, she informed her daughter that she would not be spending the night like she had done so many Sunday nights before.

Helen's plans were to drive to a town called California City, and spend a couple of days with her old friend Erma Sandler, before returning to LA on Wednesday.

Though her daughter insisted that her mom spend the night, she was no match for her mother's determination to follow through once her mind was made up.

Since the rain clouds had cleared away, and there was no further threat of anymore downpours, Helen decided it was time to get on the road.

Kissing everyone goodbye, and letting them know, that she would call when she arrived at Erma's house, Helen got into her old Buick Road master and started on her way.

She would constantly hear from her daughter how she needed to buy a new car to replace the twenty-five year old relic she was driving all over California.

Helen's answer was always the same, "Dear, I feel very comfortable and safe driving your dads old Buick. He always told me it was the safest car on the road, and I would never doubt what your father told me about cars."

It had been ten years since Helen and Stephen Fisher's marriage came to an abrupt halt, when he was struck and killed by a hit and run driver while crossing a busy intersection in downtown Los Angeles.

Suffering in the hospital for many weeks with multiple fractures and a punctured lung Stephen developed pneumonia and died suddenly.

Not being one to speed, but also not being a typical senior citizen slow driver, Helen paid close attention to the road while driving. As she traveled the dangerous highways and winding roadways through the mountain short cuts she wouldn't even turn on the radio afraid it might distract her.

About forty-five minutes outside of Bakersfield, as she was slowing down as instructed by the road signs, she felt a tremendous bump from behind her car.

Looking in the rearview mirror she saw a large raised pick-up truck, and as she tried to accelerate, it hit her again, but this time a little harder.

Trying to find a place to pull over was hopeless since the mountain wall was only one or two feet from the edge of the road, and there were no turnouts in sight.

Slowing down to a crawl, Helen tried to wave the driver by, but he refused to go around, instead he hit her car again pushing it out of control and over the side embankment.

Her car tumbled over and over, and all she could do was hold onto the steering wheel and wait until it came to a stop.

Finally ending its roll down the hill the old Buick came to rest upright, against a mound of heavy boulders and a large tree.

Just barely conscious, and very badly bruised, Helen could see someone approaching the vehicle and thought, "Thank God, someone to help."

Entering the passenger door the big stranger asked, "Are you alright Mrs. Fisher?"

"Yes I am. Did you see what happened? But how do you know my name?"

"Don't you remember me Mrs. Fisher?"

Being a retired court reporter in Los Angeles County, and a person with a great memory for names and faces, she looked at the man with a sudden fear in her eyes.

As Helen started to scream, the man put his gloved hand over her mouth, and with the other hand smashed her forehead with a rock, ending her life.

Helen Fisher's car and body were found hours later, and it was determined that she had died in a tragic accident and no further investigation was warranted.

7

Over the past couple of years Bob Ryan taught himself how to use a computer, and with a little help from a neighbor became very proficient at it. After going online, and making airline reservations for his trip to Los Angeles for the following day, the next step was to call Dorothy Metzger and let her know about his conversation with Captain Robinson.

Explaining to Dorothy what he and the captain talked about on the phone was not an easy task for Ryan, his memory, short-term memory that is, was starting to slip a little at times, but all and all, he was still pretty healthy.

As a rookie on the LAPD, Francis Robert Ryan, had a knack for remembering just about anything he read or viewed. As the years went by, and his over use of alcoholic beverages ate away at his brain cells, along with a slight Alzheimer's like condition, it became harder to remember the simplest things.

Explaining to Dorothy how he would be taking the red-eye flight out of Tampa late that night, and would be arriving in Los Angeles around 6am the next morning.

Even though she told him not to worry about hotel reservations that he could stay at her home, Ryan told her he needed the freedom to come and go at all hours of the night, but thanked her for her offer.

While packing for the trip, Ryan blurted out loud for no one to hear, "Shit, what am I going to do with Joshua?"

Joshua, a cute little pain in the ass Shih Tzu, that Ryan adopted, was his friend and roommate.

When Ryan's neighbors told him they were going to send the little barker to the dog shelter because they were moving to an animal restricted adult building in town, Ryan couldn't let that happen to the little biscuit eater so he adopted him.

Ryan and Joshua were almost inseparable, with the exception of fishing on the pier, where dogs were forbidden by the authorities.

Calling his friend and on again off again girlfriend Carol Martin, to see if she could watch the little bugger, she told him that she would rather take some vacation time and accompany him to LA.

When Ryan told her, "But Sweetheart, I need you to watch Joshua while I'm out of town."

She told him, "No problem, Joshua and my dog Misty, I'm sure will both be welcome at my daughter's home. She's been talking about getting a dog of her own since moving to Sarasota a couple of months ago she'll love it."

"But Carol, I already got my reservations to fly out of Tampa tonight at 11pm."

"Robert, give me a few minutes, and I'll call you right back."

Standing there with the phone still in his hand, Ryan thought, "Oh shit, when she calls me Robert, I know I'm going to have company on this trip I can feel it in my bones."

It had only been ten minutes when the phone rang, and knowing that it was Carol, he answered, "Ok, so what time do I pick you up?"

It was Carol on the other end, and she told him, "I called my friend Barbara Singleton, who works for American Airlines, and she is arranging for a seat for me on your flight, so pick me up at 7pm and we'll grab a bite to eat before we take off."

"Yes dear, anymore instructions?"

"Oh, and don't forget Joshua's toys and food, we can drop both dogs off on the way to the airport."

"Do I at least get the window seat Boss lady?"

"Don't be a smart-ass Robert. I'll see you at seven."

With six hours to get ready, and the addition of a traveling companion, Ryan decided to call Dorothy back and accept her offer to stay at her home while in LA, and tell her of an additional roommate.

Dorothy told Ryan, "Carol will be a very welcomed guest, someone to talk with while you're out finding out the truth."

"Dot, I will do my best to find out who murdered Leo, but I can't promise that I'll find the bastard."

"Robert, I know you'll do your best, that's all I ask of you."

"Dot, try to get a good nights sleep, see you tomorrow."

8

Pop Weston was a very likeable sixty-six year old gentleman, and happened to be a 6'5" black man living in a white mans world in Scottsdale, Arizona. The way he would put it when ever he would be around his friends and neighbors was, "Sometimes I feel like an Oreo in a box of vanilla wafers."

Harold Latrell Weston, moved to Scottsdale after his bout with cancer twelve years earlier, and he was now in remission, and enjoying life to its fullest, following a dream that he believed in.

Before moving, Harold owned a small bicycle repair shop in Los Angles, and saw a need for the same type of business in Scottsdale, after visiting his brother and nephew many years earlier.

In the beginning, when his shop first opened, the predominantly white community met him with racism and prejudice, but that soon changed because of a heroic action by the dark skinned man.

It wasn't until the bicycle shop owner saved a little white girls life, after she fell into a lake while boating, and only then was he accepted with open arms.

Fishing at the nearby lake was a pleasure Harold treated himself to each Sunday morning, and he just happened to be at the right place at the right time, and became a town hero instantly.

Roughhousing in the boat with her brother Stanley, little Brenda Styles lost her balance and fell overboard and was unfortunately a very poor swimmer.

Several people, one of whom just happened to be a local newspaper reporter, witnessed Harold jumping into the water from a near-by bridge, and pulling the drowning girl to safety.

The story ran in the newspaper for several days, and his shop became a thriving business soon after.

With the extra attention paid to his shop, Harold began putting in more hours, opening at 9am and closing at 9pm, and started thinking about hiring part time help.

A young man of fourteen named Teddy Roberts, who spent many hours at the shop, came to mind when thoughts of hiring came up.

Harold asked Teddy if he would like to work after school for a few hours each night, and learn about bicycle repairs and to help with cleaning up the shop.

The boy was very eager to except the job at his favorite store, and equally excited about the cash that he would be able to save for a new bike.

The job would only be available to him if it was ok with his parents, and Harold would have to talk with one of them in person.

After meeting with both of Teddy's parents, Harold hired him with the understanding that, for any reason his grades in school started to go down, he would have to quit.

On a wet and gloomy evening, around 8pm, the time Teddy would normally be heading home, a pick-up truck pulled into the rear parking lot of the store.

Teddy told Harold good night, and left through the front door. Halfway home he remembered that he had left his homework assignments behind the counter at the store.

Hurrying back to the store he found that the front door was locked, which was very unusual since Harold didn't close until nine.

Looking through the window he could see that someone was standing at the counter and it wasn't Harold.

Rather then knocking on the door, Teddy decided to walk around to the back door. As he rounded the corner of the building he saw a very tall and slender Caucasian man leaving and getting into a pickup truck, one with big tires and raised high off the ground.

Being careful not to be seen Teddy waited until the man drove off before he walked to the door.

Trying to open the door he found that it was locked, so he knocked, and knocked, and knocked, but no one answered.

Noticing that the bathroom window was open, Teddy climbed through and walked into the shop.

Lying behind the counter, he saw his boss Harold in a large puddle of blood, and tried shaking him, but the man was dead.

Pushing the numbers on the phone with shaking fingers, Teddy cried out when his father answered, "Daddy, please come to the store, Pop Weston is dead someone killed him."

Chad Roberts called the police and told them what his son had just revealed to him.

Hurrying to the store, Mr. Roberts met his son at the door and hugged him and told him everything would be all right, and that the police were on the way.

The Scottsdale Police Department was very thorough in their investigation, but the suspect could not be found, even with a complete description of the killer and his truck.

The town of Scottsdale was in total shock over the death of Harold Weston, and the church where his funeral was held could not hold all of the people who came to pay their last respects to the tall black man who earned the respect of so many white people.

The case remained on the books as unsolved, and unexplained.

Another senseless, unexplained murder, only this time there was a witness, Teddy Roberts. Because he was the only witness and his age, his name was kept out of the news.

9

Detective David Wells, had been with the Homicide Division of the LAPD for eleven years before his requested transfer to the San Jose Police Department in northern California.

Being a police officer who received and deserved no respect from his peers didn't bother him one bit, and sometime he would even brag about how he needed no one as a back-up no matter how dangerous the situation.

His previous assignment with LAPD had him partnered up with Leo Metzger, before Leo and Bob Ryan became partners, and it was not a paring that Leo welcomed.

Although Ryan knew Detective Wells from his horrible reputation, the two men never worked together on any cases.

Leo very seldom spoke about his ex-partner, saying only that, "I would like to let sleeping dogs lie, and he was a lying dog, a dirty cop that some day, someone would expose and put away where he belongs."

Detective Wells, a big man, stood about 6'5", weighed around 275 pounds, and in most cases would intimidate the hell out of suspects he questioned, and he liked it that way, having all that power.

Receiving a phone call around 1AM one morning, concerning a murder investigation he was working on, the obnoxious detective was told by a snitch he had been dealing with that he had to talk with him.

At first the detective told him to go screw himself, and then agreed to meet him first thing in the morning.

The snitch, a real weasel, told him, "You meet me now, or forget it, I have a message from Prescott, and I'm leaving town tonight while I can still walk on my own."

Not wanting to pass up a chance to gather information on the case he was working on, and since the name mentioned brought an immediate sense of urgency, the detective agreed to meet him. The meeting place was behind a truck stop off the interstate near his house at 2AM. Wells told him,

"You mess with me you little shit, and I'll break your skull."

As he hung up the phone, and started getting out of bed, David's wife asked him, "Where you going Hun?"

"I got this piece of shit snitch who needs to talk to me now, and he can't wait until the morning, I'll be back in a little while, go back to sleep."

Detective Wells pulled into the parking lot at the Brother's Truck Stop around 1:50AM, parked his car and walked into the diner.

First ordering a cup of coffee to go, then asked the cashier where the men's room was.

After his long awaited pee, he picked up his coffee at the cashier's register, and exited the diner.

Walking around the building he noticed someone standing at the far rear of the parking lot waving to him to come back there.

Walking at a slow pace, Detective Wells studied his surroundings as he moved away from the rear of the diner.

There were two vehicles parked along the back wall, one a dirty looking white Ford Escort, and the other a dark colored, raised up pick-up truck.

As the detective walked passed the truck he heard someone say, "I knew we would meet again Detective Wells."

Turning to see who was talking to him, Detective Wells saw a face from his past, and asked, "When did you get out of jail Prescott?"

"It's been a long time detective."

"Not long enough Prescott. Now what is it that you want?"

Lifting his hand from his side, the unexpected visitor was holding a gun and pointed it at the Detectives head.

After being instructed to walk towards the wall, Detective Wells did just what he was told. About five feet from the wall he heard the explosion of the large caliber pistol and it was the last sound he would ever hear.

While watching his prey fall to the ground, the assassin fired two more bullets into the still twitching body of the large man, smiling and saying, "What's the matter big man, got a little pain in your head?"

Looking off to the side next to the dirty car, the snitch, a creepy weasel named Robbie Charles, smiled and said, "I did good right Prescott, I got him here for you. Now don't forget the hundred you promised me."

Turning and firing one shot that entered the forehead of the slimy piece of crap that had just caused a police officer to die, Prescott said, "Paid in full."

As the raised truck drove out of the parking lot, the once very careful killer didn't notice that the truck stop cashier had seen his truck and jotted down several of the license plate numbers.

10

At 7pm sharp, Ryan was knocking on Carol's door, his little dog Joshua was on a leash by his side, and a shopping bag stuffed with doggie toys and biscuits were hanging from the retired detectives arm.

Carol answered the door accompanied by her barking little companion Casey, a chubby, but cute Chihuahua who ran into the hallway and started sniffing at his new canine friend.

Ryan smiled and said, "I hope he's fixed."

Carol smiled and said, "He sure is, but they're both males you fool."

Ryan with his witty and sometimes bazaar sense of humor responded with, "That never stopped Liberace."

Carol had one suitcase, a carry-on bag, and a shopping bag filled with Casey's toys and food.

Christina, Carol's daughter, lived only three blocks away and it only took a few minutes to drop off the two dogs and all their survival equipment.

The ride to the Tampa Airport took about an hour, and during the ride, Carol questioned Ryan about his friendship with Leo.

Trying not to come across as being to melancholy, Ryan talked about his old friend with warm feelings, explaining what their first meeting was like.

"After I ran into a dead end on a homicide investigation I was working on, I was called into Captain Hodges office. Standing in front of the Captains desk explaining why I shouldn't be taken off the case, I had Captain Hodges right in my face, calling me a sorry looking excuse for a police detective."

"Oh so you were buying your clothes at the thrift store back then also?"

Ryan smiled and asked, "May I continue smartass?"

"Continue please."

"As I looked to his right I saw Leo for the first time seated in a chair with a big smile on his face. I asked the captain, 'Excuse me Captain, but who the hell is this guy, and why is he watching my ass chewing?' The Captain said, "This is your new partner Ryan, try not to contaminate his morals." I told him, "Oh bullshit Captain, I don't need another partner." He hit me back with, "Ryan is that beer I smell on you?" I said, "Yes Sir, I had a Rummy I was questioning spill his beer on me."

He started shaking his finger at me and said, "If I find out you're drinking on the job again, I'll bust your ass right out of this department." I told him, "I'm clean Captain, I swear I'm clean"

Then the Captain said, "Metzger, meet your new partner, Bob Ryan. Now get the hell out of here, and go catch some bad guys."

Looking straight ahead at the highway in front of him so Carol couldn't see his eyes tearing up, Ryan then said, "Leo was as cleaned and pressed as a person could be, a nice smart and decent person, to nice to be a cop I thought, just an all around great guy."

"Thank you Robert, I know that was hard for you to re-live."

Arrangements had already been made by Ryan to park his car at a secure location in Tampa near the airport. They had a cab take them the rest of the way to the airport after the drive from Sarasota.

After checking in their luggage, Carol and Ryan found a nice little restaurant, had a light meal, and discussed what the plans were for the stay in Los Angeles.

As she questioned him about his intentions once in Los Angeles, it was obvious to her that Ryan's memory was not as sharp as it once was, and it took him several minutes to recall certain details that should have come much quicker.

Ryan would laugh and make remarks like, "I think I need to double up on my Ginkgo Biloba," and "Oh, that's not important anyway."

Carol said, "You keep referring to Ginkgo Biloba, what the hell is it, a memory pill?"

"Actually Carol, that's exactly what it is supposed to be, and to tell you the truth, I noticed that it does help a little, but please don't mention it to anyone."

"Robert, your secret is safe with me, but I think you should see a doctor if you're experiencing memory loss."

Ryan said, "Yeah, just as soon as we get back to Sarasota."

The plane took off on time, and shortly after leveling off at 35,000 feet, the stewardess passed out peanuts and asked about drinks desired.

Carol asked for a Vodka and Tonic, and Ryan requested a cup of coffee with real cream or milk.

The stewardess told Ryan the coffee was no problem, but only powdered cream substitute was available.

After approximately twenty minutes, Ryan had finished his coffee, and asked the stewardess for a refill, and once again asked if real milk was available.

When reminded that only powdered substitute was available, Ryan said, "Did I ask you that before?"

Carol looked at him and laughed a little and said, "That stuff was called Gingko wasn't it?"

"Yeah, I should start using Gingko as my powdered coffee additive, and maybe improve my memory."

Landing in Los Angeles, at the Bob Hope Burbank Airport, the couple quickly retrieved their luggage and made their way to the car rental agency.

Ryan had reserved a basic sedan, but because of a small mix-up, he was able get an SUV for the same rental price.

After calling Dorothy Metzger and letting her know that they had arrived, Ryan and Carol drove to the other end of the Valley to Woodland hills where she lived.

Although Ryan had spent most of his life in Los Angeles and the San Fernando Valley, he was finding it a little difficult to locate the street Dorothy lived on.

After a few minutes of Carol hearing, "Oh, now I remember," and, "When did they put that street there?"

Carol knew there was going to be some interesting things going on, and hoped that Ryan was up to the task of locating his old friend's killer.

11

On the second Tuesday of every month, Rita Hargrove had a standing grooming appointment for her little dog Shotsie, a ten-pound miniature poodle.

The little dog and Rita both seemed to look forward to the monthly visit to the Poodle Palace.

The Poodle Palace owner Betty Moore would meet Rita at 7:45am on the days of Shotsie's appointment, wait for Rita to give her little darling a kiss, and then take him inside the grooming area.

At 5:30pm, Rita would arrive back at the store after her days work at the Los Angeles Processing Company; pick up her squeaky-clean doggie and drive home.

Over the past six years, little Shotsie hasn't missed one appointment, and only once in all that time was Rita late picking up her little darling, and that was because of a traffic accident that left her car out of commission.

Never looking back after her divorce five years earlier, Rita, a very well put together woman of Sixty-two, has lived in the San Fernando Valley in Tarzana, California since her childhood.

On a wet and chilly morning, the first Tuesday in early December, Rita, loaded up little Shotsie in the back seat of her Toyota Camry, and headed for The Poodle Palace.

Arriving at 7:40am, Rita sat in her car waiting for Betty to remove the, "Sorry we're Closed" sign from the front door.

At 7:50 with pangs of nervousness, Rita walked to the door and knocked several times, but there was no answer.

As Rita turned to walk back to the car she heard, Betty calling to her from down the street.

"I'm so sorry Rita, I wasn't feeling very good and I over-slept this morning."

"That's quite alright Betty, I was worried something might be wrong, but I'm relieved to see you."

"Let me take Shotsie so you can be on your way."

"Thank you dear, I'll see you at the usual time, and please, feel better."

On the way to work, Rita stopped at a donut shop she sometimes frequented and picked up a dozen donuts for the office and a small cup of coffee for the drive.

About five minutes away from her office, having to make a panic stop by slamming on her brakes, Rita spilled her hot coffee on the seat of her car.

Pulling over to the side of the road she used the napkins provided by the donut shop to mop up her mess.

Continuing on her drive to work she was feeling like the world was against her that day.

The remainder of the day went really uneventful for Rita, and she was looking forward to picking up her little Shotsie and spending a quiet night at home.

While getting ready to leave work trying to rush a little, she opened the top drawer of her desk and quickly swept the papers she was working on into it and pushed it closed with a thud. For some reason the drawer came off its glide rail and fell to the floor.

Picking up the entire drawer and placing it on her desk, Rita looked up at the ceiling and said, "Why me, why today of all days?"

Rushing to the elevator, going down to the basement parking, the only thing on her mind was getting to The Poodle Palace, and picking up her precious little baby.

Getting into her car she didn't pay attention to the fact that the car door was not locked, thinking she must have forgotten to lock it that morning.

The second thing she didn't notice was a raised up pick-up truck parked next to her car that wasn't there when she parked that morning.

As she fumbled putting her key in the ignition, a rope surprised her around her neck held in two hands by a large man in the back seat of her car.

Struggling to get free she turned her head to the side just enough to see her attacker, screamed and held the horn depressed.

Pulling the rope as tight as he could until Rita stopped moving, he then tied it around the headrest of the seat before fleeing the vehicle.

With a smile on his face, Prescott drove his raised pick-up truck slowly out of the parking structure trying not to warrant any unnecessary attention.

Feeling like he had removed another link in his plan of assassination of persons known only to him, he disappeared into the night.

With luck from above that Rita later talked about, a security guard had heard the horn and her screams and came to her aid before she had passed away from suffocation. The guard administered CPR franticly to save her life.

The murdering madman had made another mistake, he left one of his victims alive, and he didn't know it, and she could positively identify him.

The paramedics had arrived on the scene to find Rita in a semi-conscious state being attended to by the security guard, and only moments later a police patrol car pulled up.

Not being able to talk because of injury to her neck and throat, Rita could not explain to the officers what had occurred.

The area around Rita's car was quickly roped off as a crime scene. The on-lookers were asked to please step back but to please remain for questioning.

After being transferred to the local hospital by the paramedics, Rita was admitted to a private room for treatment, observation and questioning.

Approximately two hours after being admitted Rita was visited by a Los Angeles Police Detective who introduced himself as Detective Ed Cromwell.

Although Det. Cromwell was assigned to the Homicide Division, he explained to Rita that he was involved in an on-going investigation and her attacker might just be one of the suspects he was investigating.

Still not being able to speak, Rita took the notebook and pen from the detective and wrote, Preston or Prescott, I'm not sure of his name, but I remember his face.

12

Dorothy Metzger lived on Burbank Blvd. just west of Topanga Blvd., in a section where few houses remained.

Most of the area had given way to large condo developments and apartment complexes years earlier, yet her house fit in with the surrounding buildings like it was part of the master plan.

A massive house of approximately five thousand square feet was most likely considered an oversized mansion at the time of its construction in the early 1900's.

Even at today's standards a house of that size is looked at as being quite large, but compared to some of the homes in the upper class areas, it was about normal.

Driving into the large horseshoe driveway, Carol remarked, "Not bad, amazing what one can buy on a policeman's salary."

Ryan smiled and quickly responded with, "Leo's mother and father built this house before the policeman was a gleam in his mother's eye, or a spot in his fathers balls my dear."

"I'm sorry Robert, I didn't know."

"Leo's father bought this piece of then worthless land when he first came to America, after the 1st World War, and let the property sit for twenty years before he could afford to build his dream house.

He originally purchased twenty-five acres, and as time went by he sold off building lot's, which in turn gave him funds to build what you see today."

"How long ago did Leo's parents pass away?"

"His Dad died around 1980, and I think he was about 87, and his mom lived to be 94 or 95, and she passed away in 1993."

As Carol and Ryan sat in the car talking, they didn't notice that Dorothy had stepped out onto the front porch and was standing waiting for them.

When Ryan opened his door' he heard Dorothy say, "I thought maybe you changed your mind and were going back home."

Quickly Ryan walked to the steps where Dorothy was now waiting and hugged his dear friend, as the two of them began to cry with both tears of sorrow and joy.

Introducing Carol to Dorothy, Ryan said, "Dot, I would like you to meet Carol Martin, the lady who won't let me travel alone."

"Hello Carol, It's so nice to meet a woman who can put up with this man and not be intimidated by him."

"It's very nice to meet you Dorothy, I'm so sorry for your loss."

Dorothy said, "Thank you Carol, please come inside, you can bring your bags in later, there is someone inside waiting to see you Robert."

Walking through the front door one would think you had just stepped back in time, with marble floors, beautifully carved woodwork, tapestries on the walls, and furniture the dated back to the early twenties.

Sitting in the middle of the living room on an over-stuffed winged chair, Ryan saw an old friend and quickly moved with an extended hand to greet him.

With a warm, "Hello Captain, it's nice to see you my old friend."

Captain James P. Hodges has been retired from the LAPD for just over fifteen months, but still has very good connections to the department, and if there was one person in all of LA that Ryan needed help from, it was Jim.

With a good firm hand shake and a welcoming hug, it was obvious that the two men cared a lot for each other.

While Ryan made the introduction of Carol to the ex police chief, Dorothy went into the kitchen to make a pot of fresh coffee and bring out a plate of freshly baked cookies.

As the two men started to sit, the chief said, "Before you ask, I don't think Leo took his own life either, I believe he was assassinated by some nutcase."

Before Ryan could respond, the chief asked, "Do you remember David Wells? He was with Homicide years ago, as a matter of fact he was Leo's partner before you and Leo hooked up."

"Yeah I do remember him, he was that big ass Swede with the big mouth that came over from Vice."

"Well he's past tense, they found him in a parking lot behind a truck stop in San Jose, with two bullets in the head and one in the chest, and they weren't self inflicted."

Ryan smiled and said, "Someone did the public a great service."

"I know he was rotten Ryan, but he was one of ours, he wore a badge and deserved better."

"What else do you have on it?"

"There was another victim a few feet away, believed to be involved in a case Wells was working on.

But get this; the weapon used on both men appears to be the same caliber as the one used on Leo, and even though a 357 Magnum was found in Leo's hand, we know that wasn't his gun."

"Hold it, what the hell would Leo be doing with a 357 Magnum, he only carried a 38 Snub-nose, and always said that was more then he needed, and hated carrying that."

"My point exactly Ryan, I believe he and Wells were killed by the same person, we just have to figure out by whom and why, then turn it over to Homicide."

"Have you talked to Robinson, he's treating it as a suicide, until he finds proof of something else, doesn't that suck, one of there own, and it goes on a back burner."

"I talked to him, and as soon as they get the ballistics on the bullets and the gun, he promised to let me know.

Oh, and he said if your going to go snooping around, you better stay low profile, and don't do anything to jeopardize the investigation."

"We need to sit and talk about a lot of things captain, but to tell you the truth, I've got to write more things down these days, I'm having a problem remembering too many facts, and I don't want to miss a word."

Luckily, Carol was sitting close by and had a good memory for facts, because only hours after their conversation, Ryan was not to clear on many on things discussed by he and his old boss.

13

Iris Campbell and Betty Bloomfield, enjoyed their monthly gambling trips to Las Vegas from Los Angeles each month, and loved talking about how they would break the bank some day.

Both women long time retirees, living in section eight low income housing facilities and seemingly having the Midas touch when they got around slot machines, were in their late seventies and enjoying life.

Iris would carry a small oxygen cylinder in her over sized purse when she went on long trips, the type of breathing apparatus used for emphysema, her condition brought on by many years of heavy smoking.

The two women first met while serving on jury duty in downtown Los Angeles sixteen years earlier, and stayed in close contact ever since.

Iris was the first to retire, tearfully leaving her job at the First National Bank, a job that she enjoyed more than thirty-four years.

With a little help from her daughter, Iris was able to cut through a bunch of red tape and squeeze her way into the section eight housing.

After Betty's retirement a couple of years later, from the local Target Department Store, Iris helped her friend get a one bedroom apartment right next door to her in the Northridge building.

Betty and Iris spent much of their free time with each other; they were like family, with Betty never being married and only Iris's daughter living close by.

On the first Friday of each month, both women, having packed an over-night bag, would meet in the hallway at 2pm, and then walk down the street to the senior's Rec. Hall.

The charter bus for the Las Vegas trip would start boarding at 2:30, and would be on the road by 3pm.

The Bingo game would help pass some of the five-hour road trip, with only one stop in Barstow for a stretch and bathroom break.

On most trips the bus was filled to capacity, but on this wet and cold November afternoon there was only about fifty percent occupancy.

Almost all of the passengers on the bus had made the monthly trips to Vegas before, but there were a few new faces in the group.

After a couple hours of Bingo and pleasant conversation, the bus pulled into the Barstow Station, and it was time for a stretch of the legs, a restroom break, and a small snack, then it was back on the road again.

For the next two and a half hours, the ladies talked about how this was the trip they would come home from much richer then when they departed that afternoon.

As the buss pulled into the downtown Las Vegas buss station, the passengers were informed that the return trip to Los Angeles would be boarding at noon on Sunday, and departing promptly at 1PM.

The hotel room at The Golden Nugget was complimentary from the management to the women who spent many hours each visit at the Slots in the gambling capital.

After registering for their room, Iris and Betty walked to the elevator joking about how when they own the hotel they will have the elevator much closer to the Registration Desk.

Waiting for the elevator to open the women were joined by several other people, a young couple, two elderly gentlemen, and a tall middle-aged man who had arrived on the bus from Los Angeles with the ladies.

When the elevator doors opened at the fifth floor, the couple was the first to exit, followed by the two elderly men.

Iris and Betty's room was on the seventh floor, so as the door closed Betty asked the remaining man what floor he was on, since he had not selected or pushed a button for his floor choice.

His response was, "Same as you ladies, seven please."

Betty studied the man's face for a few seconds and asked, "Excuse me, have we met before?"

"I don't think so ma'am, but it's possible, I travel around a lot."

As the ladies exited to the right of the elevator, the tall stranger walked to the left.

Walking down the hall Betty looked over her shoulder and said to Iris, "I swear, I've seen him somewhere before."

Iris laughed and said, "You old fool, he's much too young for you, now get your mind out of the gutter."

"I'm sorry dear, but I know I've seen him somewhere before, I just need a little time to recall where."

Reaching their room at the end of the hallway, they entered with the door-lock card, hung a few things in the closet, took a potty break, and quickly headed for the door.

As Iris opened the door, she was surprised to see the tall stranger standing right in front of her.

When she asked him, "Can I help you?"

The man quickly put a hand over here mouth and pushed her back into the room, letting the door close behind him.

Pulling out a metal object from his pocket, he struck Iris across her forehead knocking her unconscious. As Betty tried to scream the man grabbed her and put his hand over her mouth.

Asking her, "Do you remember me Miss Bloomfield?"

Relaxing his grip around Betty's mouth just enough so she could ask, "Who are you?" The man just smiled.

"Don't you remember me? You put my brother and me in jail. Does it come back to you now? My brother is dead, and you and your friend are responsible. Now you're going to die."

Those were the last words Betty heard, as the big man twisted her head and snapped her neck in one quick motion.

After checking to make sure that she was in fact dead, the man reached for a pillow from the bed and pushed it firmly over the now moaning Iris who offered no resistance.

Leaving the room and walking to the stairway exit, the man walked down two flights to the fifth floor where he then stood at the elevator, waiting to travel to the Casino on the main floor. There he would exit to the street and disappear into the crowd of people passing by.

Two more people had been added to a list of senseless murders, still with seemingly no connection, except in the mind of a madman named Prescott.

14

Walking back into his old station house for the first time in six years, Ryan heard a familiar voice say, "You're not on duty today Ryan, where the hell have you been, on vacation?"

"Dolan, how the hell have you been?"

The Desk Sergeant Scotty Dolan and Ryan go way back, all the way to the Police Academy, and has been working the Main Desk for the past thirteen years since he was shot in the leg during a drug bust in the Valley.

"Ryan, I knew you were coming in, Chief Hodges called me and asked me to help you in anyway I could."

Ryan asked, "Scotty, whose in charge of Homicide these days?"

"Upstairs in your old office, there's a Detective three Cromwell, who's been waiting to talk with you. I'll give him a call and let him know you're on your way up."

"Cowell, do I know him?"

"It's Cromwell, Ryan. Ed Cromwell. He came here from Oxnard right after you left, made friends with Leo, and is having a hard time excepting his death."

"Thanks Scotty, we have to go out for dinner one night before I head back to Florida."

As Ryan started climbing the stairs, the way he had done in the past, for many years before, he noticed by the time he reached the top stair that he was breathing quite heavily, so he paused a minute to catch his breath.

Standing in the doorway of his office observing quietly, was Detective Cromwell, and as he caught Ryan's eye, the one time old Warhorse stood erect, and walked towards the Detective with an extended hand.

After a brief introduction and exchange of handshakes, the two men went into the office and sat down.

Ryan, not being one to waste time, asked, "So what do you have so far on Leo's killer Detective?"

The Detective said, "First Mr. Ryan."

"Whoa, just call me Ryan please the mister is something I'm not used to hearing, especially around this place."

"Fine and you can just call me Ed."

"Leo was working on a homicide case that was on the books as unsolved, and the reason he picked it up and started checking into it was the victims name was familiar to him."

"What was the victims name Ed?"

"It was Francis Reyes, the wife of a cab driver in Los Angeles. She was found strangled in her bed at home."

"Any suspects Ed?"

"At first her husband was the number one suspect, but his alibi was solid. After months of dead ends, the investigation went to the bottom of the pile, until Leo got a hold of it and started checking out leads."

"How long ago did Leo take an interest in the case?"

"About two months before his death."

"Leo loved to keep notes on everything, especially on cases he had ideas about, even if it was not one of his. Did you find his note book on him?"

"Yes, but it's hard to make heads or tails out of some of his references."

"We'll have to get the ok from Captain Robinson to remove it from the evidence locker, but I'm sure that will not be a problem, he's looking forward to seeing you again."

"So how is he as a boss, I only remember him as a working stiff?"

"He's a real conservative, everything by the book, no bullshit, no cutting corners, and he likes to keep everything in house."

All Ryan could think of saying was, "Oh Shit."

"Oh Shit what Ryan?"

Looking at the doorway he saw a familiar face, a little older then he remembered it, but familiar.

Standing and offering an extended hand, Ryan said, "Good to see you again Bill, been a long time."

"Nice to see you again Ryan, wish it was for a different reason then a death of an old friend."

"Those Captain's bars look pretty good on you Bill, you took over where a fine officer left off."

"Jim Hodges was a fine Captain and police officer, but things are a little different around here now."

Ryan thought to himself, "I can see the shit coming now," but to his surprise the Captain shocked him.

Handing Ryan a folder the Captain said, "This is confidential material in here Ryan, make copies but the originals stay here."

Pointing at Ed Cromwell, the Chief said, "Detective Cromwell here, will help you in anyway he can, but understand this. You are not working in any official capacity except as an advisor for the LAPD, and you will not misrepresent yourself as a working police officer, understood?"

"Captain, I appreciate all that you are doing, and I will try not to embarrass you or the officers under your command."

Before another word was said between the men, Ryan stood up and said out loud, "Francis Reyes, I remember her. She was one of the witnesses in a murder case Leo and his ex partner worked on years ago. Her testimony helped put a piece of scum behind bars, if I remember right; I just don't remember the case completely."

At that point Detective Cromwell spoke up, "Excuse me, but there was the mention of a Miss Helen Fisher, does that name ring a bell also?"

"It doesn't yet Ed, but if Leo wrote it down, I'm sure it was important. For now, my memory is a little interrupted; I just need time to look over his notes."

15

After making copies of everything in the folder including Leo's notebook, studying page after page trying to connect several of the names together, Ryan said, "I got it. Helen Fisher was a Court Reporter I met many years ago during one of the cases I was involved in."

What Ryan couldn't figure out was why Leo didn't mention that Helen Fisher was a Court Reporter in LA.

He thought maybe Leo didn't know she was a Court Reporter. As thorough an investigator as Leo was, his notes left something to be desired.

For some reason only he knew, Leo jotted down names on different pages, with nothing seemingly to connect them together.

One of the items in the folder was a newspaper clipping of a homicide that took place in New

York over a year ago, and the victims name was also written at the top of a page in the notebook.

There were several other articles mentioning unsolved and unexplainable homicides, but none of the other victims were listed in the notebook.

Detective Cromwell told Ryan he would give a list of all the names in the folder to the department's computer wiz, and see what kind of cross-referencing she could come up with.

Ryan decided he would go back to Dorothy's house and look over all the material he had made copies of, and perhaps come up with a plan of action.

Before leaving the police station, Ryan thanked Ed Cromwell for all his help, and for being a good friend to Leo. The two men exchanged cell numbers and agreed to keep in touch and relay any new evidence.

Driving back to the house across the valley, Ryan kept trying to connect the names in the notebook, but nothing was clicking together.

Walking slowly back to the house, Dorothy and Carol were having a great morning, walking together on Ventura Blvd., breakfast at a comfortable little diner, and lots of warm talk.

When Ryan's name was brought up by Dorothy, concerning any romantic link between the two of them, Carol just smiled and said, "He can be so thick sometimes."

Dorothy laughed and told her, "Every time Leo and I tried to set him up for a date, he always came up with some lame excuse about why he couldn't make it that night."

Carol smiled and asked, "So he didn't date much when he lived here?"

"Date much, for a long time I thought he was gay, but even that would have shown some emotion coming out of that man. It wasn't until I got to know him better that I realized that he just kept his feelings inside and never wanted to let anyone in."

Arriving back at the house, the women found Ryan sitting on the front porch in the canopy swing, reading over the many papers he had piled next to him.

Walking up the front steps, Carol asked, "When did you get back Robert?"

"Robert, you mean someone other then I can get away with calling him Robert?"

Both women laughed, as Ryan paid little attention to either one on them.

Carol asked, "So how did your visit go at the police station."

Laying the papers down at his side, "It was an interesting meeting. I hooked up with Ed Cromwell and talked a little with Bill Robinson."

Dorothy said, "Ed has been so attentive

since Leo's death Robert. He and Leo formed a nice bond after your retirement, and when the report came out about a suicide, he refused to accept it."

Just as Ryan started to make a comment, his cell phone started buzzing, and by the forth buzz; he was able to unhook it from his belt and answer it.

It was Ed Cromwell, and as Ryan just sat and listened, giving an occasional, "Yes, ok, gotcha," then a final, "Ok, I'll call you back in a few minutes."

Looking at the women Ryan said, "We got a connection, God bless the computer age."

16

Karin Scott, a nice young lady of forty-five, a true computer geek, and an important part of police operations in Los Angeles, was about to get involved in the Leo Metzger homicide.

Karin's primary job was to cross-reference, identify, and basically link together all pertinent information supplied by the departments, to help apprehend criminals.

Detective Cromwell had worked with Karin many times in the past and found her help to be invaluable.

Categorizing all the information provided by Sgt. Cromwell, and using her superior computer knowledge, Karin came up with several connections of homicides in three cases still unsolved.

The ballistics report on the bullets of Leo's suicide, the homicides of Detective Wells, the snitch, Robbie Charles, and a storeowner in Arizona, named Harold Weston, all came from different weapons, but all of them not only came from the same manufacture, but possibly the same box.

With the help of the Scottsdale Police Crime Lab, and the LA Police Crime Lab, Karin fed in all the data into her computer. She came up with the manufacturer of the bullets, who in turn provided a metallurgy report that connected all the bullets together.

Cross-referencing all the names revealed very little more then the fact that Detectives Wells and Metzger, worked as partners for several years, and Robbie Charles was an informant used by Wells to help convict several drug dealers years earlier.

Harold Weston appeared to have no known connection to either detective, and had no criminal record, but Karin was just getting started.

Connecting all the victims together was going to take much more information, but one thing the LAPD was convinced of was that Leo Metzger's death was now classified as a homicide, and a full investigation was under way.

17

The Santa Monica Pier, located on the west coast in Santa Monica California, is visited daily by out of town travelers, and locals alike.

The pier provided fishermen with access to the bountiful supply of fish a quarter mile out off the coast.

The non-fishing visitors could enjoy the walk, beautiful sights, restaurant, and fresh air of the ocean breezes.

Many of the local residents visit the pier and surrounding beaches at all different hours, night and day.

Steve Peltz worked as a security guard and part time parking attendant at the lot adjacent to the pier, and each morning around sunrise he would greet an old friend of thirty-years who would take a morning swim before starting his day at work.

Steve's old friend, Judge Harold S. Burns, was an accomplished swimmer who in his younger days in college was on the swim team and won many metals for his long distance swimming ability.

In almost all social circles the judge was referred to as, Your Honor, Judge, or the Honorable Judge Burns, but to Steve, it was just Harry.

Each morning, even on the coldest day, the judge would take his half hour swim along the beach line, towel off, wish his friend Steve a nice day, then return home to get ready for his drive into downtown LA.

On a cold and wet January morning, just as the sun was slowly rising over the mountains to the east, and the tide was coming in, the judge had started on his first lap along the beach, when a single rifle shot rang out.

Several minutes had passed by, when the lifeless body of the judge washed a shore, going unnoticed until a jogger out for his morning run stumbled across His Honor.

Sitting in his car where he had parked the night before, and spent the past few hours sleeping off a rough night of drinking, an under cover police vice detective spotted a tall man running across the parking lot carrying a rifle, and yelled for him to stop.

Removing his service revolver from its hiding place under the car seat, the officer ran after the suspect.

As the tall man approached a raised pick-up truck, he turned and took aim with the rifle at the pursuing officer.

The detective dropped to the ground and as the suspects bullet ricochet off the ground, he returned fire striking the man in his left wrist.

Before dropping the rifle to the ground, the suspect fired once again wounding the officer in his left hip.

Hearing the exchange of gunfire Steve called 911, but before he could finish explaining to the operator what was going on, the raised pick-up truck sped by the attendants shack.

Going to the aid of the detective, Steve assured him that he got a good look at the man in the truck, and a license plate number.

Hobbling over to the rifle that had been dropped by the suspect, the detective carefully picked it up using a handkerchief. He was being cautious not to destroy fingerprints needed for evidence.

The arrival of the local police, and the crime scene investigative unit would gather together valuable information on who the suspect was, but not why he committed the crime.

The judge, who died from a single gunshot to the head, just seemed again to be another unexplained senseless homicide.

18

As information started coming in on the recent shooting of Judge Burns, it caught the attention of Detective Cromwell.

There was something about the description of the suspect's vehicle that had a familiar ring to it. An employee, who worked at the diner where Detective Wells had been shot, recalled seeing a raised pick-up truck leaving the parking lot after the shooting also.

The Ballistics report on the rifle found at the scene, at first could not be connected to any crime shootings on the books, but after a nation wide search revealed there was a connection to a shooting on the east coast, several pieces of a large puzzle were starting to come together.

The unexplained and unsolved shootings of a man named Ralph Creto in Queens N.Y., and a woman named Barbara Jones in Irvington N.J., were committed using the same rifle as Judge Burns.

The two east coast shootings had occurred over a year ago, and no new evidence had been discovered until this link with the shooting on the west coast.

The suspect had been very careful not to leave any fingerprints on the weapon, except for a couple of partial prints on two of the cartridges.

After reading about the recent shooting of Judge Burns in the newspaper, Ryan called Ed Cromwell and told him they needed to get together and talk.

When the detective asked Ryan why the interest in the Judge, Ryan told him, "Ed, there are just too many names of victims who are appearing in the paper that I'm familiar with, I don't know why, but they're all linked together."

Judge Burns was a sitting judge who Ryan had appeared before many times when he was with the LAPD, and remembered that Leo had also appeared before him as the arresting officer in several cases.

19

Sitting on the front porch of Dorothy Metzger's house with Carol by his side, Ryan was going over all the names and information Detective Cromwell had given him.

Carol read off names from the file trying to help him recall some of the people on the list. His memory of the trial long ago that Leo had told him about one night while on stakeout was slowly coming back to him.

Suddenly, Ryan looked up from his note pad at Carol and said, "Preston, no, Prescott. Yeah, Prescott, they were brothers, two pieces of shit, cold blooded killers."

Carol asked, "What does that have to do with Leo?"

Sitting back in his chair Ryan said, "Leo and his partner David Wells were the arresting officers in a case against two killers."

Trying to remember the particulars about the case, Ryan recalled Leo saying that one of the brothers got life without a chance of parole. The second brother got twenty years in a surprise lesser sentence.

"I remember Leo telling me the judge at the trial was an asshole, and the DA kept getting reprimanded for using foul language in the courtroom."

Carol continued to write things down as Ryan called Detective Cromwell.

After several rings Ed Cromwell answered, "Homicide, Detective Cromwell, can I help you?"

"Hello Ed its Ryan. I just connected some of the names in Leo's notebook, along with a possible suspect, but you need to take it the next step."

"Whatcha got Ryan?"

"Leo and David Wells were the arresting officers in a case years ago of two brothers named Prescott, I don't know their first names, but I'm sure you can find that out. One of them was convicted of murder in the first, and the other as an accomplice. The judge in the case was Judge Burns; the court reporter was Helen Fisher, and Francis Reyas was a juror."

"Ryan, I'm going to pass all the information on to our computer wiz, Karin Scott, and see what she comes up with on the Prescott brothers, and then I'll get back to you."

"Ed, you might want to check on the status of anyone else connected to that case."

"I'm sure that the records of all the witnesses and jurors are on file and easily available Ryan."

20

Rusty Baker owned a small auto and truck repair shop in North Hollywood, California.

In his younger days Rusty was a partner in one of the biggest new car dealerships in southern California.

By the age of fifty his wealth was estimated at twenty-five million, and now, only eighteen years later, his little repair shop just barely provides Rusty with enough income to pay his bills.

The years of heavy drinking, drugs, and poorly advised investments, forced the one time millionaire to sell his shares in the thriving dealership to his partner.

Purchasing and maintaining the small shop was the only thing that kept him from being destitute.

In the two small rooms above the shop, where he stored all his worldly possessions, Rusty ate, slept, and unfortunately for him, still drank very heavily, most nights passing out from cheap whiskey, wine, and anything else that helped him forget what he had become.

Over the years, Rusty had told the story about how he was sitting in the restaurant next door to the dealership, when two men in masks came in to rob the place, shot several customers and the owner.

Two of the customers died at the scene, and the owner died three days later.

Rusty had slipped out through the kitchen and as the robbers were getting into their car, he saw one of the men's faces along with the driver who had been waiting.

Being the only eyewitness who actually saw the face of one of the killers, his testimony alone gave the DA the positive identification needed for an open and shut case against the Prescott brothers.

The driver of the car was never identified or apprehended. The Prescott's maintained that they were innocent of the crimes they were accused of.

As Rusty was closing up the shop one night, looking forward to becoming very intimate with a bottle of bourbon he had purchased earlier in the day, a woman pulled up to the door and told him her car was overheating.

Not having much patience for last minute customers he chased the woman away, telling her there was an all night repair shop down the street, and he could not help her.

Watching the woman drive away with steam coming out from under her car, Rusty just laughed and said, "Damn fool woman, where was she earlier."

After locking all the doors and putting out the lights, he hurried up the stairs to his awaiting friend in a bottle.

Just as he poured himself a nice hefty drink, he heard the knocking on the door of the shop.

At first he ignored the annoying disturbance of his drinking time, but the pounding got much louder and he decided to go back down the stairs and tell the women to finally get lost and find someone else to bother.

Opening the door in a huff, and yelling, "Go away lady, I can't help you," he was surprised to see a man standing there instead of the troubled woman.

"What do you want? Who are you"?

The tall man stood there in the dark of the doorway and said, "Don't you recognize me Mr. Baker?"

"I don't know who you are and I don't care, now get the hell out of here."

With a quick smashing blow, the big man hit Rusty across his forehead knocking him backwards and on to the floor.

Lying there, bleeding profusely from his forehead, in a semi conscious state, with his eyesight blurry, Rusty asked once again, "Are you crazy? Who are you? Do I know you?"

The last words Rusty would ever hear were, "Your lying mouth sent my brother and I to prison, and you don't remember me? I'm Brandon Prescott you bastard, and my brother who's dead, sends his regards."

The big man hit him one more time in the face with the tire iron he had picked up just outside of the shops front door, checked the old man for life, and then turned and left the garage.

Outside the front door the big man picked up the gallon can of gas he had put there earlier, inserted a rag in its neck, lit it and tossed it inside the open door of the shop.

As the shop burst into a large fireball, the madman just laughed as he walked towards his vehicle.

Getting into his raised pick-up, Prescott drove away with a smile on his face feeling content.

21

Dorothy, Carol, and Ryan had just sat down to eat dinner, when Ryan's cell phone started buzzing.

Looking at the number registering on his cell phone, Ryan told the lady's it was an important call from Ed Cromwell, and he had to answer it.

As Cromwell started filling in Ryan on Karin Scott's findings, the only thing the old retired detective could think of saying was, "Oh shit, I knew those bastards were behind it."

Cromwell said, 'Not quite right Ryan.

William Prescott died in prison while serving life, without chance for parole. Brandon Prescott was released two years ago because of good behavior, and has never checked in with his parole officer and his where a-bouts are unknown."

"Ed, what about the other people involved in the case?"

"Get this Ryan, more than half of the juror's who deliberated, and found both of the Prescott brothers guilty, have turned up dead, and in each case, unsolved until now."

"What about what's her name, the Court Reporter?"

"Oh you mean Helen Fisher. Her death is still a mystery, but she was involved in the case.
The department is trying to locate everyone who either sat on the jury, or had any other involvement in the trial of the Prescott brothers."

"Ed, have you talked with Captain Robinson about all you've found?"

"He's well aware of all the findings, and has started a complete investigation into the case."

"Do you have a good description of Prescott?"

"We're sending out a full description along with photos to the surrounding states, and also putting them on the wire cross country."

"Do you think he's working alone, or with an accomplice?"

"He appears to be working alone, and his means of transportation is a pick up truck, either dark blue or black, raised high off the ground like a 4x4 with big tires."

"Has he been successful in killing all his victims or has he left anyone alive who can ID him?"

"Rita Hargrove was a juror who he tried to kill, and came damn close to it, but a security guard happened by and scared him off before he could finish the job."

"Is she local or from out of town?"

"She lives right here in Tarzana, but since the attack on her, she moved up to Ventura to live with her daughter until her attacker is apprehended."

"I'd like to talk to her if I could Ed. Would you set it up for me?"

"Sure Ryan, I'll call you when I've made the arrangements."

"Thanks Ed, nice work, I'll be waiting for your call."

After clipping his phone back on his belt, Ryan returned to the dining room table, sat down and started eating without saying a word to Dorothy or Carol.

The two women looked at him and finally Carol said, "Do you think we are going to just sit here and not ask you what the hell is going on?"

"Where do I start? The department has a very good lead on the killer, now they have to locate him"

"Who is it that you're going to talk with?"

"It's just a witness"

Dorothy asked, "A witness who saw the killer?"

"Yes"

"Yes, that's all you have to say is yes? Don't you think that's a little dangerous talking with someone who can identify the killer?'

Ryan put down his fork, looked at Carol and said, "That was my job. I did it for almost thirty years, it comes easy to me, and I know what I'm doing."

"Robert, you're right, it was your job, but now it's the police department's job."

"Miss Martin, am I going to have trouble with you, if so, you can go back to Sarasota."

"Robert, do you think I'm going to just sit here and take that crap from you?"

"Calm down Carol"

"Don't tell me to calm down. You're ready to run off to question someone who was almost murdered by some madman, and you expect me to just sit here and wait for you to return in one piece."

"Carol, what is it that you want? If it's to come with me, you can get that out of your head right now, it's too dangerous."

"Oh, and for a retired, over the hill, sixty something, burned out ex detective, its safe?"

Dorothy said, "Robert, why not take Carol along for the company. She may be able to help you in your questioning of the woman in Ventura. After all the killer doesn't know she's up there."

"Dorothy, you've got a point. Is that acceptable to you Miss Martin?"

"Oh stuff it Robert, try to leave without me."

22

At 8 am the next morning, Ryan received a call from Ed Cromwell giving him directions to Rita Hargrove's daughter's house in Ventura.

Dorothy had been up since sunrise and she had prepared a full breakfast of pancakes, waffles, scrambled eggs, sausages, and potato's.

Looking at everything she had prepared, all Ryan could say was, "Thank you Dot, all I want is coffee."

Carol said, "You just drink your coffee, I'm having some of this wonderful food that Dorothy went out of her way to prepare for us, you boob."

"Sweetheart, there is no reason to get all pissy over this."

Carol put her hands on her hips and said, "Pissy?"

"Sorry about that, I want to apologize for being such an ass for the way I acted last night."

"I'm sorry too Robert, let's have something to eat and then get on the road to, where was it, Ventura?"

After enjoying a great breakfast, and a refreshing bathroom break, Ryan and Carol got their trip under way.

While making their way through the slightly congested streets leading to the Ventura Freeway, Ryan began filling Carol in on how he was going to question Rita Hargrove. He made it clear that he did not want to worry her about her attacker, and to put her mind at ease that the culprit would be apprehended.

Driving along on the beautiful, clear, warm morning, Carol kept Ryan's attention by asking him so many questions about the surrounding area, so much that he hadn't notice the raised, black, 4x4 pick up truck that was coming up behind them.

After exiting the freeway, Ryan started looking franticly for a place that had a restroom. It seems that Dorothy's wonderful breakfast was not sitting to well with Ryan's stomach.

In order to pull into the first fast food place that he saw, he had to cut across three lanes of traffic to do so.

It was then that Ryan noticed the pick up making the same illegal turn across traffic that he made.

Not saying anything to Carol, Ryan pulled up in front of the McDonalds, turned off the engine and ran inside to the bathroom.

After relieving himself, Ryan walked slowly out of the restroom and exited the building in the rear and carefully looked around the corner of the facility.

Not seeing the pick up truck, he slowly walked to the other side of the building, and as he started to peer around the drive thru corner, he noticed the pick up in the far side of the lot.

With the heavily shaded windows, it was hard to see the drivers face, but Ryan studied the vehicle carefully, writing down the license number and making a note of the heavy damage to the front fenders and grille.

Thinking that he may just be a little paranoid, Ryan walked back into the rear door of McDonalds, and out the front, as if he didn't have a care in the world.

Carol, who let him have it with both barrels said, "What the hell was that all about? You never said a word, just parked the truck and ran inside. I hope you have some explanation."

"Sweetheart, I am not used to eating so early in the morning, and my body just decided to remind me of that fact."

"Well you could have told me what you were doing."

"We may have another problem I think we're being followed."

As Carol started to look around, Ryan grabbed her hand and said, "Don't look, I'll watch to see if he follows us out of the driveway."

Pulling out on to the street and heading back towards the freeway, Ryan casually looked at his rearview mirror and saw the pick up following far in the distance.

At the first traffic light, Ryan made a right turn and then at the first small street made another right, pulled over to the side in front of a vacant lot and watched in the rearview mirror as the pick up slowly drove past the street and then quickly accelerated.

Now it was obvious that they were being followed, but how could he know to follow Ryan?

Ryan decided to call Ed Cromwell and let him know what had just happened.

With the information provided by Ryan, the detective called the Ventura Police Department and asked them to apprehend, using extreme caution, the suspect in the black, 4x4, raised pick up truck.

All things considered, Ryan and Carol turned the car around, got back on the freeway and headed back to the San Fernando Valley and waited for another day to question Rita Hargrove.

23

Before they had traveled half way back to the San Fernando Valley, Ryan again started looking franticly for another place for a bathroom break.

Carol asked, "Have you been watching to see if we are still being followed by that truck?"

With very little emotion in his voice, Ryan asked, "What truck?"

"What truck, the black truck that was following us Robert!"

"Oh I'm sorry, my mind was concentrating on a bathroom, and soon."

"What truck? What the hells wrong with you Robert? Is your memory getting that bad?"

"No sweetheart, I just need to double up on my Ginko Biloba, you know that memory crap I take."

"Ginko bullshit, you need to see a doctor, you know, a specialist."

"I'm ok, just preoccupied with the need for a bathroom."

The truth is they weren't all right. Following far in the distance behind them, the black pick up truck was staying out of sight.

At Malibu Canyon Road, Ryan saw what he was looking for, signs for several fast food eateries, and very quickly exited the freeway pulling into the parking lot of a Burger King.

This time as he pulled into a parking space he looked at Carol, and before he could say a word, she said, "I know Robert, just go; I'll be in the 7/11 next door if you don't see me here."

Taking the car keys with her, Carol walked next door to the convenience store in search of something to help Ryan with his body function problem.

Walking in the store, the first thing that caught her attention was the aroma of burned coffee.

Looking for the cashier, she spotted her in the rear of the store near the coffee pot section. The young girl was cleaning the counter and floor, from what appeared to be a huge coffee spill that had run down the counter and on to the floor.

As the clerk looked up at her, Carol asked, "What happened?"

The girl told her that her helper had filled the coffee maker with water, turned it on, but forgot to put an empty coffee pot under it and the whole thing emptied on to the counter.

Reaching for one of the several towels on the counter, Carol started helping the girl clean and soak up some of the coffee off the floor.

A couple times as they were engulfed in the cleaning, customers had come in and were walking around the store.

One of the customers, a tall man wearing a black leather jacket, walked over to Carol and asked if she needed any help.

Looking up at the man, Carol said with a smile, "Thank you, but we have it under control."

The man asked Carol, "Are you from this area?"

Carol at that point asked, "Is there something I can do for you?"

The man said, "Just being friendly, I'll leave you to your work."

Answering quickly Carol said, "I'm sorry, it's just that my nerves are on edge."

As the man turned and walk out of the store, Ryan had passed right by him, and for a moment, stopped and turned to look at the tall man walking around the corner of the building.

Carol was now standing looking at Ryan and called to him, "I'm over here Robert helping the clerk."

Ryan turned his head to look at Carol, then back towards the front of the store, but the man was completely out of sight.

Carol asked, "Do you know him Robert?"

Ryan slowly walked towards Carol not saying a word until finally she asked him again, "Robert, do you know him?"

"That was Prescott sweetheart."

Before walking out of the 7/11, Ryan had Ed Cromwell on the phone telling him what had just happened.

The detective told Ryan he had so much more information about Prescott, including additional victims, and how the crazed killer was getting his information and location of his victims.

Asking Ryan where he was calling from, the detective told him to stay put, and he would have a patrol car there in minutes to escort them back to the valley.

Ryan said, "Don't be ridiculous Ed, I don't need a baby sitter."

"Look Ryan, I'm going to send an undercover to follow you, and possibly apprehend Prescott."

"OK, we'll sit tight. Give them my cell number and tell them to call me when they arrive, and tell them not to be too obvious about following me."

"Ryan, be careful, this guy is a sick individual, and he has killed at least ten people that we know off all ready."

"How the hell did he find out we were going to Ventura, unless he followed us from Dorothy Metzger's house?"

"I'll send a car by her house and check on her Ryan, and you keep an eye out for your back-up."

"Thanks Ed, I'll try to call Dorothy as soon as I get off with you."

Looking at Carol, Ryan said, "So how's the coffee in this joint kid?"

"Forget the coffee, what's going on Robert? What's the plan?"

"The plan is, we wait here for back-up and act as casual as possible."

"Trying to keep her voice low, Carol said, "Casual as possible? You tell me a killer was just in here talking to me, and then you say act casual as possible. Have you lost your mind?"

"Carol, an undercover patrol car will be here in a few minutes. They will contact me when they have us in sight. Then we will leave here and they will watch to see if Prescott is following us again."

"And then what?"

"If he is still following us they will apprehend him, got it, that's the plan. Now, how is the coffee?"

"I guess the coffee in the pots is fine, all I've seen so far is coffee on the counter and the floor."

Walking over to her, Ryan stretched out his arms to hug Carol, and try to assure her that everything would be ok, and under control.

Welcoming the show of affection Carol said, "I don't need to tell you do I that this scares the bejesus out of me?"

Ryan smiled, "Scares the what out of you?"

"Oh shut up and get your damn coffee."

24

The undercover car pulled into the parking lot and then exited out of the far driveway. Ryan spotted it and told Carol that their escort had arrived and it was time to leave.

Assuring her again that everything would be fine, Ryan held her hand as they walked to the car.

Making their way to the freeway on ramp, Carol couldn't help but fidget in her seat and look in all directions as they drove on.

Heading back into the valley, Ryan pointed out some of the buildings that were set into the mountainsides along the freeway, all the time watching his rearview mirror keeping an eye on their escort far to the rear.

The Black pick-up truck never appeared during the twenty-minute drive, but Ryan knew it was just a matter of time before Prescott would show his ugly face again.

Arriving at Dorothy's house, Ryan was surprised to see Ed Cromwell's car parked in the driveway.

Carefully and slowly Ryan got out of his car and had instructed Carol to wait for him to check and make sure everything was okay.

As Ryan slowly walked up the front steps, the front door opened and to his relief, Ed came out onto the porch.

Ryan smiled and said, "I've got to tell you Ed, I was a little worried seeing your car here when I pulled up, not knowing if that bastard had gotten here first."

"Dorothy's fine Ryan, but I'm going to request an officer be assigned for additional security in the area."

Carol had opened the car door and stepped out and asked, "Is everything okay here?"

Ryan waved to her and said, "All is fine sweetheart."

By this time, Dorothy had joined them on the porch and said, "Coffee's on, and Lunch will be ready in a few minutes."

"Ed, you told me on the phone that you had more information on Prescott?"

"Let's go in and sit and I'll fill you in on some real strange findings."

Dorothy looked at Carol and said, "Dear, would you help me in the kitchen for a while?"

"Dot, you said the coffee was ready?"

"Yes Robert, you two sit, and I'll bring in the coffee. How do you like yours Ed?"

"Black is fine Dorothy, thank you."

As the two men sat down, Ryan asked, "So what do you have Ed?"

"Well, the first thing you need to know is that Prescott is not working alone on his crime spree. He has a family member who has provided him with information on the victims he has killed, and possibly committed two of the murders. The rifle that was used in the killing of Judge Burns, Barbara Jones, and Ralph Creto, had a second set of fingerprints on it that were not Prescott's."

"Who the hell did the mad man recruit?"

"Several prints belonging to a Grace Davis were also lifted off different parts of the weapon. Mrs. Davis's name before her marriage to Stanley Davis was Grace Ann Prescott."

Ryan sat forward in his chair and asked, "An ex-wife?"

"No Ryan, his sister. Get this. Grace Prescott did eight years with Uncle Sam's Army, before becoming an employee of the IRS.

While Stationed at Fort Campbell Kentucky, Sergeant Prescott became extremely proficient at fire arms use and repair, before transferring to Quartermaster Accounts and Records."

"Have you located the sister?"

"Not only have we located her, but she is being picked up as we speak from the IRS office in Los Angeles."

Sitting back in his chair a little more relaxed to hear the new information, Ryan said, "She obviously has some connection to some of the murders, seeing that her prints were on the rifle."

"That's exactly what we're going to find out Ryan."

"Well Ed, let's get over to the Station house, I don't want to miss any of the questioning."

Carol who was listening to all the new information said, "Robert, if you think you're going without me, you're crazy."

"Carol, I wouldn't think of leaving you behind."

25

Mel's Drive-in diner is located on Ventura Blvd. in Sherman Oaks, California. For the most part, a fine place to eat if you like good home cooked food at a fair price.

The history of Mel's goes back many years, when driving your car into a parking space, turning off your motor, and in most cases a pretty young girl would walk up to your car and ask you what you would like to eat.

Over the years of changing times, the days of the Carhop waiting on drive-up customers has gone the same way as the Dodo Bird, and it doesn't seem to be coming back.

Chester Baranski lived with-in walking distance of Mel's, and made it a point to eat dinner there every Monday night between five and six pm.

Chester had many favorite meals he enjoyed eating with his coffee on the side, but his all time favorite was the Lumber Jack special, it just seemed to hit the spot for him.

The Lumber Jack Special consisted of three eggs, potatoes, three pancakes, and a nice size ham steak.

A waiter he had gotten to know as Double D, whose real name was actually David, took real good care of Chester each time he came in. David made sure he was his server, if for nothing else, the good conversation, and always a nice tip.

On this particularly cold and dark Monday night, while the diner had only a hand full of customers, Chester had walked down Kester Avenue from the hillside above. He entered through the front door, waved and said hello to David, and sat down at a booth in the rear of the diner.

David, without even asking, brought Chester his cup of coffee, creamer, a handshake, and a smile, and asked how his old friend had been.

After going over all the somewhat boring things that he dealt with that week, Chester ordered his Lumber Jack special, with eggs over easy.

Sitting and reading a book he had brought with him, Chester only managed to read two pages before his food was brought to the table.

Starting to eat, he looked around and noticed that there were still very few customers in the diner that night, but knew it was still early and most of the customers came in after six, when he would be long gone.

Sitting at the tables at the front of the diner were two women, one fairly young and one closer to retirement age.

In the front corner booth there was a tall middle aged man, busy reading a newspaper and sipping his coffee.

At the counter there were three teenagers who just couldn't stop complaining that there was no modern rock and roll in the jukebox.

Finishing up the last of his meal, Chester called David over to the table, handed him a twenty-dollar bill and said, "This should more then cover it my friend, and you keep the change."

Thanking him, David said, "Till next week Buddy, you take care." And like every Monday when Chester was ready to leave, David would ask, "How about a coffee to go?"

"Maybe next time David I've had my fill of caffeine for the night."

Picking up his book, Chester slowly walked to the front door, exited, and proceeded to walk through the large dark parking lot at the rear of the building.

During Chester's conversation with David, he hadn't noticed that the big man from the front booth had left the diner a short time before him.

Walking in the parking lot between a Ford Explorer and a Chevy pick-up truck, he was surprised as the door to the pick-up truck swung open and the tall man stepped out and blocked his path.

Chester said with a smile, "I'm sorry friend I didn't notice you in the truck."

The man answered, "I'm not your friend, but I am here to see you."

Chester once again spoke up and said, "Look Buddy, I don't know who you are, but I don't like this."

"I'm not your Buddy and I'm not your friend, and you don't remember me, do you?"

"I'm sorry, but no, I don't remember you, I don't believe we've ever met."

Just then the big man grabbed Chester by the front of his shirt and said, "My name is Brandon Prescott, does that rattle your memory?"

Chester thought silently for a while, and then said, "Oh my God, you're that murderer we sent to prison for killing the people in the restaurant."

"You and the rest of your group decided that my brother and I committed murder, and you sentenced him to die and me to rot in jail, well you were wrong."

With one quick movement, the big man lifted his right hand and displayed the large hunting knife he was holding, and then with a flick of his wrist cut

Chester's throat from ear to ear, watching as the life drained from the crying mans body.

Dropping the bleeding man to the ground, the tall man pushed Chester under the Ford Explorer and drove off at a slow pace as if nothing at all had occurred.

Chester's body was not discovered for another hour, until the woman who owned the Explorer came out of the diner.

Since there were no witnesses, Chester Baranski's murder went on the books as unexplained and unsolved, but only for a short time. It would soon be connected to the string of murders committed by Brandon Prescott.

26

Grace Davis was seated in the #2 Interrogation room accompanied by Officer Brenda Reese, when Ed Cromwell, Ryan, and Carol, arrived at the Van Nuys Police Station.

Because questioning had not yet begun, and Mrs. Davis had not been charged with any crime yet, she had chosen not to have an attorney present.

With the arrival of Detective Cromwell and the assistant District Attorney John Rogers, Mrs. Davis was informed of her rights and that the conversation was being recorded. She in turn refused legal representation once again.

With the assistant DA, Ryan, and Chief Robinson seated in the adjoining room, Ed Cromwell first asked Mrs. Davis, "What exactly is your relationship to William and Brandon Prescott?"

"Detective Cromwell, you know damn well what my relationship is to them, they are my brothers."

"It's strictly for the record Mrs. Davis."

Sitting in the chair with her arms folded across her chest, Grace Davis said, "William died in prison, and Brandon was released from prison two years ago. Is that what you want to hear detective?"

"Mrs. Davis, do you know the where-a-bouts of your brother Brandon Prescott?"

"No I don't detective, we were never very close."

"When was the last time you saw your brother?"

"It was about four years ago, just after William died. I visited him in prison."

"That was the last time you had contact with him?"

"Yes it was."

"Did you ever own a 30-30 Remington bolt action rifle, or do you know if your brother Brandon owned one?"

Grace Davis sat silent for a moment and then said, "I think I would like to speak with an attorney now, I have nothing else to say."

At that point all the questioning came to a stop, because once a suspect requests legal representation, no further interrogation is permitted without violating the rights of the suspect.

While Mrs. Davis remained in interrogation room #2, the assistant DA, the Chief, Ryan, and Ed Cromwell all went for a conference in room #4.

Carol, who had been sitting patiently in the hallway, called out to Ryan as he started to enter the second room, but to no avail.

Getting up from her chair, she walked over to the now closed door and knocked, then entered, asking, "Robert, can I have a word with you?"

"I'm sorry Carol, Prescott's sister just decided she needed a lawyer. DA Rogers, this is Carol Martin, my close friend and confidant."

"Hello DA, it's nice to meet you."

"It's John Rogers Carol, and I'm pleased to meet you also."

Looking at the chief, Carol said, "Hello chief, nice to see you again."

"It's very nice to see you again Miss Martin, but I'm sorry you'll have to leave the room."

Before any further conversation went on, another detective entered the room, excused himself and asked to speak with the chief privately.

Stepping out of the room for only a few minutes, the chief and the detective returned and the chief said, "Everyone, this is Detective Bruce Johnson, and he has some additional information about the case your involved in."

"Hello everyone, I'm sorry for the intrusion but I believe I have something that is connected to your investigation. Last night a homicide took place in the parking lot of Mel's Diner on Ventura Blvd. in Sherman Oaks. The victim was a Chester Baranski. When we ran a check on the victim, we found that he was on a Locate and inform list of Karin Scott's. From what we have been able to find out about Mr. Baranski, he was a juror on the Prescott brother's trial."

Without thinking, Ryan said, "Holy shit, the bastard got another one. We've got to find him and stop him."

The DA asked, "Have the remaining jurors been located and informed on the situation chief?"

"John, if they haven't been, they will be immediately, I promise you."

Ryan looked at both men and said, "There aren't that many left, and he seems to know where to find them all."

Carol spoke up and said, "It's easy, his sister works for the IRS, they can locate anyone. The IRS has access to information on just about everyone in this country."

27

Approximately two hours had passed since Grace Davis had requested to have an attorney present before she would answer any further questions.

Being a government employee of the IRS, Mrs. Davis knew she was entitled to legal representation at any time it was needed.

Derek R. West, attorney at law with the very old and distinguished firm of, Whitehill, Whitehill, Reese, and Cohen, of Los Angeles, answered her call.

After a brief conversation with his new client, Mr. West asked for the DA, to return to the table and find out just what he has on his mind.

It was decided by the DA that Ryan and Carol Martin would be able to view and listen in to the interrogation from the adjoining room.

Mr. West and John Rogers were familiar with each others work, but had never gone head to head in any cases in their past.

After a quick introduction, Mr. West was very direct and said, "OK, let's cut to the chase. What is it that my client is being charged with?"

The DA said, "Your client has not been charged with anything yet Mr. West, but that could soon change if she refuses to cooperate in our investigation of her brother."

"What is it exactly that you need from my client, Mr. Rogers?"

Looking at his notes, the DA asked, "Mrs. Davis, have you ever owned a rifle, specifically, a Remington 30-30 bolt action type?"

"Yes I did, many years ago."

"Where is that rifle today Mrs. Davis?"

"I have no idea Mr. Rogers I haven't seen that rifle for over twenty years."

"Would you be surprised to hear that that weapon was used in several execution style homicides?"

"Yes I would"

"Would you also be surprised to hear that both yours and your brothers fingerprints were found on that weapon after it was dropped at the scene of a recent homicide?"

"No I wouldn't. If it was my rifle, of course it would have my fingerprints somewhere on it, but like I already told you, I haven't seen that rifle in over twenty years."

"How do you explain your brother's fingerprints being on that weapon?"

"I have no answer for that, except, that my brother may have borrowed my rifle many years ago and used it for hunting or target practice."

"I'll ask you once again Mrs. Davis do you know the location of your brother Brandon?"

"No I don't Mr. Rogers."

"Would you tell me if you did know where he was?"

"No."

"Mrs. Davis, do you mean to say that you would protect your brother, even though he has murdered so many innocent people?"

"Yes."

"Your brother William died in prison paying the dept for the murders he committed."

"My brother William never killed anyone he died an innocent man in a hell hole of a prison."

"Councilor, I recommend that you inform your client, that if she dose not agree to co-operate in this investigation, I will press charges against her for aiding and abetting a murder suspect, and I will lock her up until she makes bail, which may not be for a couple of days.

After a whispering conversation between her and her attorney, Mrs. Davis said, "I will cooperate with your department completely."

"One other question comes to mind Mrs. Davis. Did you use your position at the IRS to locate witnesses and jurors who convicted your brothers in their trial twenty years ago?"

Once again the whispering between Mrs. Davis and Mr. West went back and forth, until the attorney spoke up and said, "My client and I need a little private time to discuss just how certain questions need to be answered."

The DA responded immediately by saying, "I would expect your client to answer truthfully councilor."

"Mr. Rogers, we all would like the truth to come out, but we have to make sure innocent people are not harmed along the way to truth and justice."

As the DA, Chief, and Ed Cromwell were leaving the room, the detective turned and asked, "Just how high did you qualify with a rifle in the Army Mrs. Davis?"

The attorney spoke very quickly and said, "Don't answer that Mrs. Davis."

"I don't mind I'm sure you already know detective, I qualified as an Expert Marksman."

"One other thing, what did you mean by your brother William was an innocent man?"

"My brother William was not with Brandon when he robbed that restaurant twenty years ago."

Her attorney spoke and said, "That's quite enough Mrs. Davis, don't say another word, we need to talk now."

Walking out of the room, DA John Rogers stared at Grace Davis, and she stared right back at him.

After about fifteen minutes, Mr. West informed the DA that there would be no more questioning until the following day, and wish Mrs. Davis released.

The DA informed Mr. West, "Mrs. Davis will remain a guest of the state until it has been decided whether to charge her or release her."

"And when do you think that decision will be made?"

"It will be decided when we are confident that she has been completely truthful in her answers to our questions."

"John, you know as soon as I leave here I'll be filing a writ for her immediate release."

"Derek, file your writ, she's not going anywhere tonight."

28

Sitting on Dorothy Metzger's front porch, Ryan sipped his coffee and stared at the front gate, almost in a trance like state.

Ryan's emotions seemed to be traveling from one extreme to another, feeling bad that his involvement in this investigation has lasted so long, and kept him away from his home. On the other hand, he has taken away any doubt that his ex partner and friend Leo had committed suicide.

As Carol walked out of the front door she asked Ryan, "Robert, how long have you been out here?"

As if she had not spoken at all, Ryan just continued to stare at the front gate, remaining in a frozen state.

"Robert, are you all right?"

"I'm fine Carol, just going over so many scrambled things in my head."

"Have you been taking your memory medicine Robert?"

"You mean my Ginko dear? Yes I have, and it has helped to keep my memory as sharp as a rubber bumper."

Carol said, "Robert lets go into the kitchen and talk this over."

As they walked Carol asked, "So what's troubling you dear?"

"Why do you think Prescott's sister is so adamant about the other brother not being involved in the robbery twenty years ago?"

"Maybe he told her he wasn't there."

"Yeah, like he would really admit committing a robbery and killing someone in the process."

"Ok, let's look at it another way, do you have all the facts on the robbery twenty years ago?"

"No I don't it hasn't all been made available to me."

"Why not Robert?"

"Some of the files aren't complete."

"Why aren't they complete?"

"Twenty years ago everything was done by hand, most of the reports were typed but many were hand written."

"So that means there were a lot of incompetent detectives taking down the information?"

"Watch it Carol, that's going a little too far."

"Well, let's pack up and go home then, we're done here."

"No, I'm not ready to pack it in yet there are a lot more questions I want answered."

From outside Ryan could hear some talking on the porch. It was Dorothy, and she yelled out, "We have a problem Robert."

"What is it Dot?"

Without hearing an answer from her, Ryan started walking towards the front door, and then stopped in his tracks.

Walking through the front door was Dorothy Metzger, with Brandon Prescott right behind her, holding a gun to her head.

Prescott spoke and said, "What questions might they be, Mr. Ryan, maybe I can answer them since I'm here?"

Ryan put his coffee cup on the table next to the chair and calmly said, "Let the lady go Prescott, she has done nothing to you."

"Ryan, I like things just as they are."

"Prescott, why are you killing all these people?"

"Because they killed an innocent man, and they have to pay for my brother's death."

"From what I read of the trial transcript, it was a no-brainer, your brothers gun was the murder weapon, it was his car used in the getaway, and when he was arrested, the police found some of the stolen items in his apartment."

"You fool. My brother was never there; he was past out in a drunken stupor in his apartment while we went to the restaurant, and I used his gun and someone else drove his car."

"Why didn't he speak up at the trial and expose the other guilty participants?"

"One of them died after the robbery, and the other got away."

"Why didn't you expose them to save your brother?"

"Enough of this bullshit, you wouldn't understand, now where is that bitch Rita Hargrove living?"

"Rita Hargrove, haven't you killed enough people already?"

"Unless you want to see this woman die also, you will tell me what I want to know. Where is Rita Hargrove?"

"You followed us to Ventura. You followed us to the address we had for Miss Hargrove. It was a vacant lot. I don't know where she is, the police have her in protective custody."

"You're lying to me, I'm warning you, I'll kill her, she means nothing to me, and then I'll kill this tramp you have sitting with you here."

Carol stood up and said, "TRAMP, you piece of shit. You murdered all those innocent people, and you call me a tramp."

"Shut her up Ryan. Shut her up or I'll kill them both."

As he tried to calm down Carol, Ryan noticed Detective Cromwell's car pulling into the driveway, and so did Prescott.

The crazed Prescott pushed Dorothy Metzger to the floor and said, "I'll be back Ryan, and next time I may kill you all."

With that, Prescott locked the front door, and ran through the house and out the back door, jumped the low fence, got into his truck and drove away.

Unaware of what had just taken place, the detective walked up the porch steps and knocked on the door.

Carol being closest to the door opened it and said, "Your timing is perfect detective, thank you."

29

Prescott's pick up truck was long gone by the time Ryan explained to Cromwell what had just taken place. The detective immediately called in the attack and requested a black and white at the scene for security precautions.

First questioning Ryan and then the two women, Ed Cromwell expressed a sincere concern for them.

Within minutes there was an order to proceed with caution in the apprehension of Prescott, an order that was already in effect, but know it was followed by his last breach of the law.

The visit to Dorothy Metzger's home was not just a social call by the detective, but one to inform Ryan that Grace Davis had disappeared, and that there was new evidence connecting her to two homicides on the east coast.

After making sure that everyone in the house was ok, Ed Cromwell informed them all that Karin Scott has been busy on her computer checking out all the information on homicides connected to the Prescott family.

As he read from his notes he said, "In April of last year, Prescott's sister took a trip to the east coast, specifically, New York and New Jersey.

While in New York, she rented a vehicle from a small car rental agency that specialized in high-end vehicles, like BMW's, Cadillac's, Premium SUV's, and Mercedes. The vehicle she rented was a two-year-old gray, four-door Mercedes. Before the shooting of Ralph Creto, a gray, four-door Mercedes was spotted parked just down the street from the Perez home.

One week later in Irvington New Jersey, another shooting occurred of Miss Barbara Jones, and before her murder, a gray, four-door Mercedes was one of the vehicles spotted in the area across the street from her store."

Dorothy Metzger asked, "Ed, who are these people that were murdered?"

"Both of the victims were jurors who convicted the Prescott brothers twenty years ago Dorothy."

"So Ed, you're saying that Prescott's sister did the shooting, and not Brandon Prescott?"

"That's right Ryan. We can put Brandon at the time of the first homicide in his doctor's office with the flu, and the second shooting he was in his doctor's office getting a complete physical."

"Do you have any idea where she took off to?"

"No Carol, but we're working on it."

"What about the remaining jurors Ed?"

"Ryan, eight of the twelve jurors have been killed, and we suspect the Prescott's of their murders.

Two others died of natural causes, and one has not been located yet.

Which leaves Rita Hargrove, and she had an attempt on her life that was botched, and a security guard saved her, so she is in protective custody.

Including Leo Metzger, Detective Wells, the snitch Robbie Charles, Judge Burns, and a Court Reporter named Helen Fisher, this madman and his sister has killed more then a dozen people."

Carol spoke up and said, "Why has it been so hard to locate him or his truck?"

"My guess Carol is, he has had twenty years to plan this out in some form, and since his brothers death four years ago, he has had a chance to perfect his plan."

"He must be living somewhere."

"We have passed out a complete description and the latest photographs available."

"He must park his truck in a garage somewhere Ed, a vehicle like that would be easy to spot parked on the street, wouldn't it?"

"Yes it would Carol, and all the departments have been put on alert to keep an eye open for his vehicle, the problem being that he could be parking it on private property out of sight."

"Ed, what about gas stations, can they be notified to watch out for that truck?"

With a smile on his face, Ed Cromwell told Carol, "This is a big city, with thousands of gas stations Carol."

"Yeah, but he seems to be driving around this valley more then anywhere else Ed, that's got to make him easier to find."

"That still leaves hundreds of stations to notify."

"And you have how many police officers in police cars Ed?"

Ryan looked at Ed Cromwell and said, "She's got a good idea Ed, and it wouldn't take that much to put together some flyers with a description of the vehicle and the suspect and have the officers in the patrol cars pass them out to the local gas stations."

Ed Cromwell said, "I'll contact the Chief and see what we can do; it sounds like an idea that might fly."

Dorothy came over to Carol and hugged her, saying, "I would watch it if I were you Carol, your starting to think like a detective, Ryan must be rubbing off on you."

Ryan had this little smirk on his face, so Dorothy asked him, "Robert, what do you think? Is she starting to act like a detective?"

Ryan's expression seemed to change, kind of a lost look, and then he asked, "Why would you ask me that Dot?"

As everyone looked at Ryan, Carol walked over to him and put her hand gently on his cheek and asked, "Are you alright Hon?"

Ryan just seemed to stare across the room and said, "I'm ok Carol, just a little tired."

Ed Cromwell spoke up and kind of broke the icy feeling in the room and said, "Great idea Carol, I think we have a place for you in the department."

30

Chris DeMarco enjoyed the cool weather of the northwest town on the outer edge of Portland Oregon. His move to the area came about after his wife of thirty-seven years and he divorced.

Chris's ex, Linda, had a severe love affair with alcohol, and after her long bout with alcoholism that left her a basket case in the care of the state, the un-happy couple separated for twelve years, followed by a long drawn out divorce.

Chris had been a long time employee of the RTD Bus Co. in Los Angeles California, putting in thirty-five years before he semi-retired to Portland.

Having sold his house in California, which he and his wife had paid off many years earlier, it gave him more money then he needed to purchase the comfortable two-bedroom trailer home he and his dog Mandy shared in a comfortable trailer park on the outskirts of town.

Being a man of seventy, and looking more like he was sixty, Chris had the attention of many of the younger widows of the area.

Keeping himself in good physical shape was very important to Chris, ever since he took a part time job as a security watchman at a local lumber yard.

Shortly after his arrival in Portland, Chris enrolled in the Armed Response Security Academy, where he earned his license to be an armed security guard, which gave him many job opportunities.

Being a single person with only his dog to take care of, and himself, restrictions on working hours were non-existent, and he preferred working the graveyard shift giving him his daylight hours to do other things.

The rain had been falling all day and into the night, a very common day in the Portland area. It was a night that left Chris with chills and a slight fever, he could not wait to get home to have a hot shower, a cup of tea, and curl up in his waiting bed.

Returning home after his eight hour shift at the lumber yard at 5:30am, he found that the front door to his trailer had been pried open, and his faithful companion Mandy was nowhere in sight.

Entering the trailer very cautiously, Chris heard Mandy barking from the rear room.

Walking slowly to the door he opened it and his loving pet jumped up to greet him. After a few seconds of petting and panting, Mandy began to growl.

Turning to see the reason for her unusual behavior, Chris noticed a woman standing by the kitchen table with a gun pointed in his direction.

The woman instructed him to put the dog back in the room and close the door.

In the darkness of the early morning, and the shades and curtains closed up tight, it was hard to see the woman's face clearly. She told him to sit at the table and pay attention to what she had to say.

He asked her, "Who are you?"

She said, "You wouldn't know my name, but you know my brothers names, William and Brandon Prescott."

Chris's mouth opened, and he gasped, "Oh my God."

Her response was, "You better pray to God, because he is the only one who can help you now."

"What do you want with me?"

"I'm here because William died in prison."

"So why have you come after me? Your brothers were convicted murders, who had to pay for what they did."

"My brother William did nothing, and you helped sentence him to die for a crime he didn't commit, and now you're going to die."

As the woman sat down across from Chris at the table, Chris slowly unzipped his heavy coat, and unbuttoned the top button of his uniform shirt.

As the woman spoke of all the horrible people who helped convict her poor brothers, Chris slowly removed his snub-nosed 38 special from its quick clip holster on his belt with the table hiding his moves.

The conversation went back and forth, with meaningless attacks on Chris's judgment as a juror at her brother's trial so many years ago.

From speaking in a calm and soft voice, Chris all of a sudden yelled, "MANDY, NO."

When the Woman turned her head to look for the dog, Chris lifted his gun above the table and fired two shots into the chest of his captor.

Falling backwards off the chair to the floor, Grace Prescott Davis let out one small grunt, before she fell silent.

First checking to see if the woman was indeed dead, he pushed aside the gun from her hand, leaving it on the floor next to her body.

After calling the police, Chris opened the bedroom door, hugged his dog, and then sat back down at the table.

Within minutes, his neighbors were at his front door seeking to find out what had happened.

Chris realized that only because of his physical conditioning and sharp reflexes, he was alive, but still wondered why she wanted to kill him. In all her ranting, Grace Davis never explained the real reason she knew her brother was innocent.

It only took forty-eight hours for all the information to arrive at the desk of Detective Ed Cromwell, and he couldn't wait to pass it on to Ryan.

Ryan's response was, "One murdering bastard down, and one to go."

The detective told Ryan that once Prescott finds out that his sister was dead; he would most certainly seek revenge.

31

Ryan's visit to Los Angeles had already been much longer then he had planned. Carol was getting her chance to spend more time with the crotchety old retired detective then she felt was fair. Although they got along quite well most of the time, they were both in need of their own space, and couldn't wait to return home to Florida.

Dorothy Metzger was really happy to have the company of the Floridian couple, but also felt like the stay was hopefully coming to an end.

Each day there was something that she had to remind Ryan to do. If it wasn't to turn off lights before going to bed, close and lock the doors, stop leaving the milk out on the kitchen table, walking around in his underwear, or putting the toilet seat down when he left the bathroom, it was just Ryan's memory loss that was becoming an annoying problem.

Ed Cromwell was also having a difficult time with Ryan's memory, with having to remind him of things they had discussed several times, and hearing a response, "I know, I know, I'm not stupid, I remember that," when it was obvious that he didn't remember it at all.

Being forever grateful for their comfort and caring in her time of need, following Leo's death, Dorothy suggested that Ryan possibly see a specialist in memory loss before his return home.

Ryan did not take it nicely, and informed Dorothy that he is dealing with it in his own way.

A couple of days had passed by since hearing the news about the shooting of Grace (Prescott) Davis, and Ryan decided it was time for he and Carol to return home, and let the police take care of apprehending Prescott.

Making the airline reservations online, he informed Dorothy that he and Carol would be flying home in two days, but would stay in close touch, as if they had never left.

Dorothy said, "Robert you know I care for you very much, your being here through this tough time is so appreciated. If I start to feel alone, I'll leave the toilet seat up some night, so I can feel that cold porcelain bowl on my butt in the middle of the night when I have to go," and then smiled.

Sitting on the sofa between Carol and Ryan, Dorothy held hands with her two friends and said,

"Having you both here has been a blessing, and I only hope after all of this is over, I can come and visit you both in Florida".

After making a phone call to Ed Cromwell, Ryan told both women that there was no new news about Prescott, so he decided he had to do some laundry and start packing.

The three of them went out to dinner that night, and went to a movie afterwards, a movie that Ryan had no say so over its content; a chick flick was his only comment.

Back to Dorothy's house around midnight, the three of them stayed up talking until 2am.

After saying goodnight to each other, Ryan said he was going to stay up a little while and watch an old movie on the TV, but would be sure all was secure before turning in.

While making himself a cup of instant coffee, Ryan thought he would write down a few notes about his thoughts on the whole Prescott incident.

Remembering that his notebook was out in the car, he went out to retrieve it, leaving the back door unlocked after his return.

Settling in nice and comfortable in the over-stuffed recliner, with his coffee and notebook at his side, he turned on the TV and prepared to enjoy watching an old favorite movie, Casablanca.

Just as the song, "As time goes by", was being sung by the old piano player Sam on the TV, Ryan heard Dorothy say, "Robert, you left the kitchen door to the back porch un-locked."

"Sorry, I went to the car to get my notebook."

"Robert, with that madman still on the loose, we are going to have to be more careful."

"I'm really sorry Dot, my mind is just not thinking clearly these days."

Kneeling down on the floor across from him, Dorothy reached out her hand to hold his and said, "Dear, I remember when my mom went through memory loss, it was devastating to everyone around her."

"I'm fine Dot honest, just a little tired."

"That was my mom's go to answer, every time I had to remind her of something she forgot to do."

"I promise when I get back to Sarasota, I will make an appointment and have myself checked."

Walking into the room, Carol asked, "Is this a private meeting, or can I sit in?"

"Hi Hon, Robert and I were just discussing possible plans for the next couple days."

"So what do you have in mind Dorothy?"

"I thought I would cook a nice dinner for you two later tonight."

Ryan said, "Dot that would be great. Ed Cromwell wants to take Carol and me out to lunch today, and say his goodbye."

Carol asked, "Robert, have you checked on the return tickets for tomorrow night?"

"Everything's set Carol. Now I think we should all get to sleep, it's going to be a busy day tomorrow."

32

Approximately ten miles away from Woodland Hills, at the Van Nuys Police Station, the Desk Sergeant picked up the phone and said, "Good morning, Van Nuys Division PD, Sergeant Stearns speaking, may I be of some assistance?"

In a very low voice, a woman said, "Sergeant, my name is Brandy, and I work at the 24 hour gas station on the corner of Coldwater and Magnolia in Valley Village."

"Yes ma'am, what can I do for you?"

"One of your officers dropped off a picture of a pick-up truck, and I think he's in the station now."

"Ma'am, please stay calm, speak up and give me a little more information. What is your address?"

"I just told you, Coldwater and Magnolia. Too late, he's coming to the booth, bye."

It took approximately ten minutes for the first patrol car to pull into the station, and a couple more minutes for the next four to seal off the area, but unfortunately the pick up truck was gone.

Through questioning of the cashier it was learned that it was not his first visit to that station, that he was a frequent customer.

Brandy told the questioning officer that she remembered seeing the truck in the early hours of the morning, usually before daylight.

33

With a slight glimpse of the morning sun shinning through the drawn curtains in Ryan's bedroom, the clock radio went on playing the final notes of a jazz song called, 'Cast your faith to the wind.'

Ryan, just lying there, noticed that Carol had gotten up and had not returned to the bedroom.

The radio announcer had just started his weather forecast for the day, when Ryan decided to get out of bed and get ready for the day ahead.

After his 3 S's that he called them, (Shit, shower, and shave) Ryan walked downstairs to the kitchen, where he found Dorothy and Carol sitting at the table enjoying coffee and conversation.

"Good morning Robert, have a seat and I'll get you a cup of coffee."

"Good morning Dot, thank you, coffee would be nice."

"Do I get a good morning also Hun?" Carol asked.

"I'm sorry sweetheart, good morning."

Dorothy looked at Carol, smiled and said, "It's so nice to see him in such a nice mood for a change."

Ryan just flashed a sarcastic wide smile and said nothing.

Unclipping his phone from his belt, Ryan called Ed Cromwell to check on the plans for lunch, but got more information then he had planned on.

The report of Prescott's appearance at the gas station in the early morning hours, was sitting on Ed Cromwell's desk when he came in that morning.

"That's great Ed soon you'll be closing in on that bastard."

"Ryan, what time does your plane take off tonight?"

"Midnight Ed, but we have a lot to do between then and now. So what time is lunch, and where do we dine?"

"Are you ok with Deli food Ryan?"

"Sounds good to me, I'll ask Carol"

"You'll ask me what Robert?"

"Deli ok for lunch with Ed?"

"That's fine Robert."

"Ok Ed, Deli it is, now where?"

"How about Fromins Deli in Encino, you remember Fromins don't cha Ryan?"

"Ok, noon at Fromins, we'll see you there."

After getting of the phone, Ryan told the women about Prescott being spotted at the gas station in Valley Village, and that it wouldn't be long before he was behind bars if all goes right.

Dorothy and Carol had decided that dinner that night would be a nice prime roast, mashed potatoes, carrots, and spinach, followed by apple pie.

While Carol went upstairs to dress, Ryan sat down in the living room with his coffee and the newspaper.

On the front page, in the lower right corner, the story of a woman wanted in Los Angeles for questioning, was shot to death by a man she was herself trying to murder.

The incident took place in a trailer park in Portland, Oregon, and a thorough investigation was under way.

Ryan thought, with the story hitting the Los Angeles papers, Prescott was sure to see it, and would seek his revenge for his sister's death.

What Ryan had finally accepted, was that his days of chasing the bad guys was over, and the younger new breed of police could handle everything without his help.

By the time Carol had come back down, an hour had passed, and Ryan was dozing in the over stuffed chair.

Carol looked at Ryan and said, "Fine, I'm upstairs making myself pretty for you and you're down here taking a nap."

Ryan smiled and told her, "How could you improve on a true beauty, you're perfect just the way you are."

"What's got into you today Robert?"

Dorothy walked in and said, "He's just showing his human side, and I think it's wonderful."

Carol asked, "Dot, what are your plans for today?"

"I'm going shopping at the market, and then I think I'll bake that apple pie, it sends a nice aroma all through the house that lasts a long while."

Ryan said, "Have fun Dot, we'll see you later, if you think of anything you need, just call, you have my number."

"Robert, please ask Ed Cromwell if he would like to join us for dinner, it should be around sixish."

"Will do Dot, have fun."

Leaving the house, Ryan and Carol were in such a happy state of mind, that they drove down the street not noticing Prescott's pick-up truck parked in the parking lot of the condo across the street.

34

The lunchtime crowd at Fromins Deli was unusually small, but the noise level in the building remained quite high because of the acoustics created by the structure.

Retired Chief Jim Hodges had joined Ryan, Carol, and Ed Cromwell for lunch, and because of the noise level in the building it took three rings on his cell phone before Ryan realized he had an incoming call.

Looking at the caller ID, Ryan said, "Excuse me please, it's a call from Dorothy Metzger."

Answering, Ryan said, "Hi Dot, what's up?"

"First Detective Ryan, It's not Dot, you know me better as Brandon Prescott."

"Second, Mrs. Metzger has decided to accompany me to another location other then her home."

"Put her on the phone let me talk to her Prescott."

Those words being heard silenced everyone at the table, and all eyes were on Ryan.

"Don't you hurt her in any way you bastard."

"Mrs. Metzger is safe for now detective."

"Prescott, I am no longer a detective, but I promise you, if you hurt that woman I will hunt you down and cut your heart out my self."

"Enough of your promises Ryan, this is what I want from you, and if you co-operate you may get to see your friend again. I want to know where Rita Hargrove is. I don't want any bullshit from you, just her location.

"I don't know her location Prescott."

"Well you better find it if you want to see your friend alive and breathing again. I will call you later. Don't fail, or you know what I am capable of.'

With that, the phone went dead, and Ryan just stared at it for a moment.

Looking at Ed Cromwell Ryan said, "Prescott has Dorothy, and he wants Rita Hargrove's location, or he will kill her."

"Robert, we can't go back to Florida under these circumstances.

"No Carol, we're not going anywhere until Dorothy is home safe and that bastard is in jail or in the morgue."

Ed Cromwell asked, "Ryan, Prescott said he would call you back when?"

"He didn't say exactly Ed, just that he would call me, and I better have the information he wants."

Jim Hodges spoke up, "Ed, I think you had better contact Chief Robinson and fill hill in on the latest, and I also think lunch is over."

"I agree Chief I'm calling my boss now."

35

In a North Hollywood garage, in an area under heavy re-development, Prescott sat at a makeshift desk with his feet propped up on two milk crates, eating a sandwich and sipping on a bottle of beer.

The garage was located behind a larger building once used for manufacturing of truck bodies, but now fenced in and destined for demolition to make way for a new mall.

A small window-less room with a steel door, once used for tools and equipment storage, was located only a few feet from Prescott's sitting area. The room now contained a semi-conscious Dorothy Metzger, with hands and feet bound.

In the front section of the building that was large enough to accommodate several vehicles much larger then his own, Prescott's raised pick-up truck took up hardly very much space to park at all.

The garage at one time had been used by transients as sleeping and living quarters, but now had been taken over by Prescott. After he secured the building with his own locks and traps for anyone entering unannounced, he could come and go knowing that his hiding place was safe. It was made very clear to anyone who wanted to invade his space, that they would be met with extreme violence which would result in their death.

Out of the many who had used the building in the past, only one was befriended and partially trusted by Prescott, a society outcast named Drexel Hunt, a piece of vermin fitting of the madman's friendship.

Allowed to occupy a space in the garage in exchange for his scouting, silence, and services to Prescott, Drexel saw nothing, cared about nothing, and didn't want to know anything concerning the big man's business.

Although the afternoon sun provided much warmth and light to the outside, the inside of the garage remained dark and damp, and only sparse light came through the several dirty and boarded up windows on the north side of the building.

A large candle provided light for Prescott at his desk as he studied a map of the Portland Oregon area.

Planning his next move after he finished with Rita Hargrove, Prescott had already found out the address of the trailer park and location of Chris DeMarco's trailer. The information had been passed on by Prescott's sister before her visit there and eventual death.

As the moans and groans of Dorothy Metzger filtered through the door of her imprisoned room, Drexel Hunt was instructed to give the woman water but pay no attention to her begging for help.

36

Returning to Dorothy's house, Ryan and Carol were joined by Ed Cromwell, Jim Hodges, and a crime scene investigating team. Although apprehending Prescott was the responsibility of the police, Ryan was trying desperately to come up with a plan to catch the elusive criminal.

Sitting out on the screened front porch as the crime scene guys did their work, the three men and Carol talked about possible scenarios that would seem real enough to trap Prescott, and not put Rita Hargrove in any danger.

Turning over Miss Hargrove in exchange for Dorothy Metzger was completely out of the question. Exposing her location was also not an option that could be considered.

Ed Cromwell suggested that a policewoman might be put in place to impersonate Miss

Hargrove, and be under close surveillance while they set a trap for Prescott.

Ryan asked, "You mean set her up in an apartment and just give Prescott her address Ed?"

"No, nothing that obvious, but it's an idea."

Captain Hodges put in his two cents, "What about letting him discover where she is, he seems to have an analytical mind, crazy as a loon, but he is resourceful."

"What do you have in mind Chief?"

"Ed, you would have to clear it with your boss, but I think I have a plan."

"Ryan, you told me that Prescott followed you up to Ventura, when you and Carol drove up to see Rita Hargrove, is that correct?"

"Yes Chief, but we never got to meet with Miss Hargrove."

"But Ventura, you led him to Ventura, and he believes that Rita Hargrove is in Ventura, right?"

"Right"

"He's going to be contacting you again, and what you need to do is sometime during your conversation, let it slip out, without being obvious, that Miss Hargrove is under the care of a physician. Maybe something like in her present condition she may not make it to her next birthday. In any case, that she's not well from his attack on her and has been in and out of consciousness and may not be long for this world."

"Where are you taking us with this Chief?"

"Detective, if your boss goes for it, maybe the capture of Brandon Prescott, or the end of him."

"I'll call him Chief and try running your plan by him."

Just as Ed Cromwell started to punch in his captain's cell number, one of the investigators came out on the porch and said, "All clear guys, you can go in any time."

37

Four days had passed since Dorothy Metzger's kidnapping and her daughter, son-in-law, and granddaughter had arrived in town from their home in New Mexico.

Dorothy's son Paul was expected to arrive from New York that afternoon, and all of them would be staying at Dorothy's house.

Ryan had cancelled the plane reservations for the return trip to Florida, and he and Carol were planning on moving to the Sportsmen's Lodge Motel in Studio City.

Although the Metzger's made it clear that they wanted Ryan and Carol to stay at the house, the ex detective said he needed the solitude of the motel for his thinking process, and piece of mind.

Ryan's last conversation with Prescott had also been four days earlier and searching for Dorothy had turned up absolutely nothing, with no one coming forward with any information. It wasn't until the morning of the seventh day, when a report came through from the Portland Police Department. There had been an attempt on the life of Chris DeMarco which was not successful, but left Mr. DeMarco with a bullet wound to his shoulder.

While working at the lumberyard where he was a security guard, he was making his rounds checking the fences, when he was shot from a vehicle parked across the street from the main gate.

An off duty police officer spotted the pick up truck leaving the scene, and chased it for several miles until loosing sight of it a heavily wooed area.

At first report, Mr. DeMarco was assumed deceased, but the paramedic's were able to revive him, and is now in stable condition.

After talking with Detective Ed Cromwell, it was decided that Chris DeMarco's condition would be kept confidential, and a story of his demise would be reported to the newspaper with a copy story going to the Los Angeles area newspapers.

With hopes dwindling for Dorothy Metzger's safe return, it had not stopped the Los Angeles Police Department, with co-operation from Ventura Police Department, from putting together an elaborate sting operation to catch the elusive Brandon Prescott.

The ex-chief Jim Hodges, had put together an ingenious plan, based on the insane drive Brandon Prescott had to exterminate everyone that he believed was responsible for his brother's incarceration and eventual death.

Figuring that he would stop at nothing, other then his own death, Prescott was sure to bite at the bait supplied by the crafty detective's.

38

Rookie patrolman Bobby Carlson and Officer Alex Ragus, were parked in an undercover car at the Ralph's supermarket parking lot adjacent to the 76 gas station on Magnolia Blvd, and Coldwater Canyon in Valley Village.

At approximately 2:45 AM, Patrolman Carlson shook his dozing partner and said, "Alex, Alex, wake up, I think this is our guy. Isn't that the pick up we're looking for?"

Brandon Prescott had just pulled into the gas station and was walking up to the cashier's booth.

After calling into the station house, the officer's were given their instructions, "Do not apprehend. Follow at a safe distance to his next location."

After filling up his truck with gas, and paying the cashier, Prescott drove out of the gas station on to Magnolia Blvd. and headed east.

Allowing the pick up truck to get a safe distance away before the officers started to follow, the men stayed in contact with Detective Cromwell who had now been called at his home.

The pick up truck drove at a steady forty miles per hour, obeying all the stoplights it had encountered. Two blocks after crossing Vineland Avenue, Prescott made a left turn onto a very dark street in the highly commercial area.

At that time in the morning there was very few vehicles on the road, so the officers had to be very careful not to be spotted.

Officer Ragus informed his partner that he was very familiar with the area, and instructed him to pull over and park the car he then got out and proceeded cautiously on foot.

Watching as the pick up truck pulled up in front of the old deserted building at the end of the street, the officer's saw Prescott get out of his truck and first open the chain link gate, then the door to the garage.

After Prescott returned to his truck, and drove inside the building, the officer watched as a second man came out of the building, closing the gate and then the garage door.

Returning back to their car, Officer Ragus said to his partner, "Bobby, this guy is dangerous, but if we all play things right, his ass is done for."

Arriving at the location, Ed Cromwell had already started to put together an assault team, and with the location of the building being where it was, it was one way in and one way out, Prescott was boxed in and that was good.

The condition and location of Dorothy Metzger not being known would be a big factor on how the assault on the building would be carried out.

39

The SWAT assault team had arrived on the scene in North Hollywood, and was starting to take up positions on the surrounding streets, tightening up the area around the garage where Prescott was hiding.

The area residents being know to contain a high concentration of gang population was quickly becoming aware of the police infiltration. The police presents caused great concern to those people living close by with outstanding arrest warrants on them.

With many of the paranoid gang members fleeing the location, it caused an unusual amount of activity on the normally quiet street, which caught the attention of Prescott.

Sending Drexel Hunt out to find out what all the commotion was about, the assistant to Prescott only made it half way down the street before being apprehended by the police.

Watching his stooge get picked off the street, like an apple off a tree, Prescott knew he was in great danger of being arrested.

With all the candle light in the building first being extinguished, Prescott unlocked the barn type doors to the garage, started his truck, put it in drive, and accelerated, pushing the doors open and then crashing through the chain link fence.

Before reaching the end of the street on to Magnolia Blvd., the raised pick up truck had been hit by over a dozen gun shots, but the truck never stopped, as it made the turn and disappeared heading east.

Not known to the officer's doing the shooting, that two of their shots had found their mark, wounding Prescott in the neck, and another in his left leg.

Although patrol cars had tried to give chase, by the time they had gotten underway, the elusive murderer had once again avoided capture.

Less then five minutes had passed by and Ed Cromwell was inside the garage, and opening the door to Dorothy Metzger's cell.

As the detective kneeled down at her side he touched her face, and her eyes opened, and she said, "Hi Ed, I knew you would find me, but I'm so tired."

The first call Ed Cromwell made was to request a Paramedic at the scene, and the second call was to Ryan, to let him know that Dorothy was safe, and would be on her way to the hospital to be checked out.

Ryan, not ever known for being a religious person said, "Thank God, that's the best news. Thank you Ed."

Letting everyone know that Dorothy was safe, Ryan then said, "But the murderous bastard got away."

40

Ryan and Carol had decided to spend at least one more week in California, for several reasons. Making sure that Dorothy recovered from her abduction by Prescott was the most important of all. Hopes of seeing the mad man caught by the police or eliminated by some other force of nature ranked second.

Because of their last minute cancellation of the flight back to Florida, it would now cost Ryan double for his return flight, but waiting one week would lower the cost.

Four days had passed since Dorothy's return home, and her Daughter and family were leaving for their home in New Mexico, now that mom was safe and sound.

Dorothy's son Paul decided to stay for a couple of weeks to keep his mom company, and use some of his saved up vacation time from the company he worked for.

There had been no sightings of Prescott, and no phone calls until the day before Ryan and Carol were supposed to leave for Florida, and when he called Ed Cromwell he asked for Ryan specifically.

Although the detective told him all deals had to be made through him, Prescott said, "It's Ryan, or no one, get him to the phone now."

The detective told him he would have to contact Ryan and let him know, and asked, "How does he get a hold of you?"

"You have him by your side tomorrow at noon, and I'll call you, got it."

Before the detective could answer, Prescott had hung up.

Immediately calling Ryan, Ed Cromwell told him, "Your not going home just yet Ryan, Prescott will only deal with you, and you alone."

41

At twelve noon, Ed Cromwell's phone began to ring, and with Ryan at his side he answered, "Ok Prescott, Ryan is here, but understand this, I am in charge, and all arrangements go through me. Got it?"

"Yeah, yeah, I'll be careful not to bruise your ego, now hand the phone to Ryan."

"Ok Prescott, this is Ryan, what do you want?"

"First of all, I know where you and your dear friend Miss Martin live in Florida. Where your dead friend Leo's daughter lives with her family in New Mexico. I even know where the queer son of Metzger's lives in New York, and I can get to them any time I want. Do you understand me?"

"You bastard. What is it that you want?"

"I want Rita Hargrove, she is the last person who has to pay for my brother's death, and I'm not

166

going to stop until she pays for what she did. After that, you'll never hear from me again."

Listening in on the conversation, Ed Cromwell was writing notes and showing them to Ryan, some of which Ryan just waved off and shook his head, no. The one note that Ryan shook his head yes to was the words, "Ventura Hospital Sting."

Ryan started raising his voice at Prescott and acting confused and erratic with his answers.

At one point in the conversation, Ryan just blurted out, "For God's sake you madman, the woman is in the hospital, just barely hanging on to life. Why can't you just let her die in piece surrounded by her family?"

In the background, Ed Cromwell said, "Enough Ryan, why are you telling him that?"

It was all choreographed and played out well by Ryan and Cromwell, knowing that Prescott would take the bait.

Prescott's response was, "Thank you for telling me just where I could find her."

Ryan said, "She'll be moved Prescott, you'll never find her."

As the detective kept on yelling at Ryan in the background, Prescott started laughing and said; "I'll see you all in hell some day."

After the connection was broken, Ryan said, "Ok Ed, you better work quick because you know, he's heading for Ventura."

"The arrangements have already been taken care of Ryan. When Prescott calls the Ventura County Hospital, he'll find out that Rita Hargrove has been transferred to a private nursing home, called Maiden Care Facility if he pressures hard enough. That facility is a set up sting operation on the outskirts of town."

"Ed, this better work, because I think you'll only get one shot at him."

"Ryan, the entire facility is staffed with police officers, and the Ventura SWAT team will have the building completely surrounded. One shot, I don't think so. We'll try our best to capture him, but if he resists, he will never leave the compound alive."

Ed Cromwell's cell phone once again rang, and it was Prescott.

"Do you think I'm a fool detective?"

Ed Cromwell was at a loss for words, so all he could think of asking was, "What are you talking about Prescott?"

"Did you think I wouldn't find out?"

"Alright, stop with the questions, and get to the point."

Cromwell looked at Ryan, who had no idea what was going on.

Thinking that Prescott some how found out about the sting operation in Ventura, Ed Cromwell asked, "Did you hear something that I don't know about Rita Hargrove?"

"Rita Hargrove.

Who the hell is talking about Rita Hargrove?"

"Then who the hell are you talking about?"

"Chris DeMarco, he's not dead after all, you and the press have been lying and trying to deceive me."

With sweat now running down his temples, the detective lied his ass off and said, "Listen you dumb shit, I only know what I'm told, and as far as I know, Chris DeMarco died in the hospital from your gun shot wounds."

I'll tell you what detective. After I end the misery of Rita Hargrove, I'll go back up north and make sure I did a good job on DeMarco."

Without another word spoken, Prescott cut off the conversation.

After pushing the END button on his cell phone, Ed Cromwell looked at Ryan, smiled and said, "He's taking the bait we better get going to Ventura fast."

As they headed for their transportation, Ed Cromwell made his first call to the Ventura Police Department to inform them that Prescott was possibly on the way there.

The detective's second call was to Captain Robinson to fill him in on how things were progressing, and that he was headed for Ventura.

42

As Ed Cromwell and Ryan entered the freeway on-ramp, Ryan's cell phone started buzzing away. Looking at the caller ID, he could see the call was coming from Carol.

Answering he said, "Yes dear. Ok Carol. I'm sorry I haven't stayed in touch with you. Carol please, this is not the right time for this. Ed and I are on our way to Ventura, if all goes as expected, it will all be over soon. Yes, I'll call you and let you know. Yes, I love you too. I'll call you when it's over. Goodbye dear."

Looking at Ryan and smiling, Ed Cromwell said, "All you need is the wedding ring buddy, because you're sure hooked into that relationship."

"Ed, there will be no wedding ring, and the only relationship is that we are very good friends."

"If you say so Ryan, but from what I've seen and heard she has the ring through your nose already."

With about a half-dozen calls made to the Ventura PD, the hospital, Lt. Randle of the SWAT team, and The Ventura Maiden Care Facility, everything seemed so solidly in place.

The Ventura Maiden Care Facility had closed its doors over five years earlier, due to poor management. The building now belonging to the city was a perfect location for the sting operation the Ventura PD had arranged.

With only two possible entrances to the parking lots, decoy vehicles were parked at each entrance.

One vehicle was an old X-Ray trailer, with writing and pictures of a medical nature on its sides that fit right in with its surroundings. Inside the trailer were a half-dozen of the finest sharpshooters with the Ventura SWAT team.

The second vehicle was a large step-van that appeared to be used for building maintenance, but in reality, it was a SWAT truck with five Expert Marksmen equipped with high-powered scoped rifles.

The personnel inside the facility were police officers posing as doctors, nurses, and patients.

As extensive and elaborate as this plan seemed to be, Brandon Prescott's ability to escape captivity has warranted the extreme action.

While in-route to the facility, Ed Cromwell received a call, informing him that a phone call inquiring about Rita Hargrove had been made to the Ventura County Hospital as predicted.

After much questioning by the caller who had pretended to be a family member, he was told that Miss Hargrove had been transferred to the Maiden Care Facility. The caller, who gave his name as Jason Hargrove, Miss Hargrove's brother also asked for directions to the facility.

Arriving at the Maiden Care facility, Ed Cromwell and Ryan joined the officers inside the building and waited in the cafeteria area for the arrival of Prescott. Unfortunately, many hours had passed, and there was no sight of the elusive killer. The plan that seemed too perfect to fail was at a complete standstill, with no sightings and no calls.

It was 10:15pm when Ed Cromwell told Ryan that he had about all the coffee his kidneys could process, and with Prescott being a no show it was time to head home. The Chief of the operation from Ventura PD told him he would be contacted if Prescott showed his ugly face.

Driving back into the San Fernando Valley, the two men traveled quietly, with the windows open and the cool night air circulating through the car, and the clear skies with stars sparkling above.

Driving up and over the Conejo grade, on the Ventura Freeway, a sudden rise in temperature was felt by both men, and Ryan said, "I had forgotten just how hot the valley gets compared to Ventura."

Waiting just outside of the front lobby of the Sportsmen Lodge after receiving a call from Ryan, Carol watched as the traffic on Ventura Blvd. drove by. The sky was clear and there were many stars shinning above, but Carol missed her wonderful Florida sky and longed to return to her home.

When Ed Cromwell's car pulled up in front of the building Carol walked over to the car to greet them. Ryan looked at her and said, "The bastard didn't show."

Watching Ed Cromwell drive off Carol said, "I want to go home Robert. I really miss my home and my dog."

Walking slowly heading to their room, Ryan took Carol's hand in his and said, "It' will be over soon and then we can both go home."

Carol told Ryan of the earlier conversation she had had with Dorothy, "Robert, Dorothy wants us to move back to her house and won't take no for an answer."

"I'll call her in the morning sweetheart."

"You don't understand, she wants us there tonight, she's waiting up for us now. I've already packed up our stuff, we just have to check out and drive there."

"Tonight, we can't wait until the morning?"

"She's waiting for us tonight, I suggest you call her."

The call to Dorothy Metzger was short and not so sweet, and within one hour Ryan and Carol were heading for Woodland Hills.

43

Sitting at a desk in room 211 at the Regent Motel in Van Nuys, Brandon Prescott was planning out his next move.

The ten o'clock news had just started on the TV when the deranged killer got up from his chair and walked out the door to the parking lot.

Prescott's truck, which was parked in the space nearest to the back alley driveway, had been vandalized and the tires slashed, which sent the tall man into a rage.

Walking into the motel office, Prescott asked for the manager and was met with sarcasm, by a half drunk old man who didn't like the idea that his favorite TV sitcom was being interrupted.

Being a person who did not like being put off or talked to in an abusive manner, Prescott slowly walked around the counter, grabbed the old lush by the front of his filthy t-shirt, and smacked him in the side of his head with a paper weight he had picked up from the desk.

Dropping the bloody unconscious man to the floor, the big man looked on the desk and the key rack for keys that might fit one of the vehicles parked in the spaces in front of the office.

Finding a set keys marked, 'Toyota pick-up,' Prescott walked out of the office and tried them in the small red truck parked in the spot marked, 'OFFICE PARKING ONLY.'

With the results he had hopped for, Prescott now had transportation to continue on his mission.

44

Although Dorothy Metzger was so happy to welcome the couple back to her home, she told them, "Now I know I can sleep in safety."

Ryan and Carol had decided to take a short walk around the neighborhood to try and relieve some of the tension, and after about thirty minutes it seemed to be a wonderful success.

Arriving back at the house, and each of them being much calmer then when they started on their walk, they decided to have a cup of tea before turning in for the night.

For Carol, the chamomile tea seemed to do the trick, making her feel like the next thing on her agenda was a soft warm bed and a date with the sandman.

For Ryan though, his nerves were still on edge, and he decided to stay up a while longer and watch a little nighttime TV.

After giving Carol a kiss good night, Ryan went into the kitchen to see if there was anything he might be able to fix for himself to compensate for not eating all day, before settling down in front of the television.

Dorothy had told him that there were leftovers from the afternoon barbecue in the garage refrigerator if he was interested, and bottles of iced tea on the patio in a cooler.

Ryan told her that he wasn't interested in either, but thanked her for the idea.

After eating a few cookies from the cookie jar, Ryan changed his mind and thought he would check the garage refrigerator just for the hell of it to see if something struck his fancy.

Loading up his arms with barbecued chicken, potato salad, coleslaw, and baked beans, the overly hungry old fart carried it all inside and started heating things up in the microwave.

Carrying his large hoard of now heated food into the living room, he remembered the iced tea and went out to retrieve a couple of bottles to wash down his meal.

Bending down to pick the bottles out of the cooler, was the last thing Ryan remembered until he woke up sitting in the passenger seat of the little red Toyota pick-up truck driving down the freeway. Prescott had climbed over the wall in the rear of the yard and quietly pried open the door of the rear porch and hid in one of the dark corners.

With a seat belt strapped tightly around him, and his hands and feet taped securely with duct tape, Ryan heard a laugh followed by, "Well it's about time you woke up detective."

Ryan turned his head slowly and responded with, "I've told you before you asshole, I'm not a detective, and I've been retired for years."

"You'll always be a detective in my eyes Ryan."

"Where are you taking me Prescott?"

"You're going to help me settle things with Rita Hargrove, and then Ryan I'll decide what to do with you."

"Why don't you leave that woman alone and let her die in her own time, she's very sick and near death as it is."

"Let's just say I'm going to help her get to her final destination a little sooner."

"And then what?"

"You mean after I torture or kill you? I think I'll take a trip up north, I hear it's a lot cooler now then when I was there on my last visit."

Exiting the freeway at Johnson Rd., Prescott pulled to the side of the road and looked at a piece of paper that he had written directions on for the location of The Maiden Care Facility.

Looking at Ryan, Prescott said, "I know you could probably direct me right to the place, but as you can see, I came prepared."

45

Hearing the slight commotion coming from downstairs, Carol and Dorothy both went down to the kitchen, and found the back door to the patio wide open, and Ryan was nowhere to be found.

The ice chest that contained the iced tea was open, and spots of what appeared to be blood were on the tan patio flooring tiles.

Carol first tried to call Ryan's cell phone, with no response. She next called Ed Cromwell.

After assuring Carol that he would do everything he could to locate Ryan, the detective called the Ventura Police Department to alert them that the killer may be on his way to the Maiden Care Facility, but to be aware of a hostage in the vehicle.

Getting on the freeway heading to Ventura took Cromwell only a few minutes, and because of the late hour, the traffic was very sparse.

Locating the road leading into the Maiden Care Facility, Prescott pulled over near a group of trees and bushes and parked the truck.

Studying carefully what he could see of the parking lot, Prescott told Ryan, "You know what Ryan, I don't like the way it looks out there. They wouldn't be setting some kind of trap for me would they Ryan?"

"Fuck you asshole."

Prescott said, "Not many vehicles here for a place this big."

"Good shithead, let's get out of here."

Prescott smiled and said, "I think I'll take you with me just to be on the safe side, you know what I mean Ryan, just for insurance."

Getting out of the truck and walking around to the passenger door, Prescott opened the door and removed the tape around Ryan's ankles, undid the seatbelt and pulled him out.

With the moon almost full Prescott holding on to Ryan's arm pulling him along had no trouble at all making his way across the parking lot.

The building was an old looking all brick structure that had two floors not counting the basement. The Ventura PD had authorized the electrical power to be turned on so everything appeared normal.

Approaching the side entrance with extreme caution, Prescott watched through a window to observe the movement inside the building.

Noticing that only one person, a nurse, was the only one in sight, he decided to quietly enter the building.

The first room Prescott came to on his left as they walked slowly down the hall was room # 124.

Opening the door slightly and looking in, the killer noticed that the room was bare of all medical equipment, including a bed and chairs.

Following in order on the same side of the hall, was room #122, and was also empty of all normal hospital equipment.

Slowly and quietly moving down the hall towards the Nurse's Station Desk, Prescott looked in several of the other private rooms, noticing that none of them were occupied.

As he reached the desk, and the nurse looked up from the book she was reading, Prescott asked, "Rita Hargrove, which room is she in?"

Studying both men and not seeing Ryan's hands taped together because of a towel covering the tape, but not missing a beat, staying right in character, the nurse said, "Sir, it is long after visiting hours, and there are no visitors permitted until 8am in the morning. Besides sir, there is no one here by that name."

Prescott responded, "I'm sorry, I just got into town, and she is my only sister, I would just like to see her for a minute or two. I know she's being secretly kept here."

"It's against the rules sir, but I'm sure under the circumstances if you have some identification?"

Removing a gun from under his shirt, Prescott said, "I'll just be a minute, thank you. Tell me which room or die here, your choice."

Putting her hand up to here mouth she said, "Oh my god sir, she's in room 105, please don't shoot me."

Prescott said, "Too late lady."

Using all his weight Ryan pushed Prescott to the side before he could fire his weapon, as both men fell to the floor.

The female officer, posing as the nurse, quickly rolled off her chair and crawled to the exit door behind her.

Prescott laughed and said, "Run bitch, I'm not here for you anyway."

While Ryan remained on the floor, Prescott got to his feet. Without much effort he kicked Ryan in the side of his head and watched him pass into unconsciousness. Pointing his gun at Ryan, Prescott decided for some reason not to shoot him at that time and started walking down the hall to room 105.

By the time Prescott walked halfway down the hall to room 105, two officer's had crawled through the emergency exit door and dragged Ryan to safety.

Entering room 105 slowly, Prescott saw that the privacy curtains hanging from the ceiling were drawn and surrounded the bed.

Removing a straight razor from his pocket, Prescott slowly opened the curtains, and to his surprise, the bed was empty.

Realizing that he had been set up and led into a trap that would most likely lead to his death, Prescott removed his gun from his belt and looked out the window.

Noticing that there were all kinds of movement in the parking lot, Prescott exited the room and opened the side door to his right leading to the outside on the opposite side of the building that he had entered.

A beam of light from a high powered searchlight shined in his face, followed by the words, "The building is completely surrounded Prescott, lay down your weapon's and come out with your hands over your head."

Quickly firing several shots at the lights Prescott then started running to the other end of the hall, finding the same situation there with a large search light aimed at the exit. His next attempt he returned to the center desk noticing that Ryan was gone, and opened the door behind the Nurses station. Jamming it open with a chair a light quickly illuminated that exit also.

Turning out all the lights he could find switches for, Prescott next looked to the front door, and decide that it would be his best means of escape, if at all possible.

After firing a half dozen shots out of the rear door at the lights, Prescott very quickly ran to the front door, opened it and charged out of the building.

The bright lights came on and he was lit up like a star on a Broadway stage. The expert marksmen who had the front of the building well covered, took the killer down with just a couple of shots, but as he tried to get up, he was hit with several more, ending the rain of terror that resulted in so much loss of innocent lives.

Leaning next to a police car and seeing Prescott hit the ground in a mass of gunfire made Ryan smile as he gave a fist pump to the sky saying, "Justice finally."

Several miles away, at her sisters home, Rita Hargrove received the phone call that she had been waiting for, advising her that her life was no longer in danger.

Ryan was able at last to witness the death of the madman who had taken his dear friends life. Although it was closure in a way for him, he knew there were many families who would never have that same closure.

Ed Cromwell, who had arrived at the scene just before the fireworks started, called in the report to his captain, who was glad to hear it was over and additional lives were not lost.

The chief told his detective that evidence had been uncovered that Grace Prescott Davis had been the third person along with her brother who committed the robbery and murders so many years earlier. Her brother William was truly an innocent man but to protect his sister's identity he went to prison.

Ryan called Carol on Ed Cromwell's cell phone, and let her know that he was safe, and of the killer's demise. He then asked her if she would start packing so they could get the hell out of town and go back to Sarasota where things were a little more quiet and peaceful.

Carol said, "You damn old fool, I have been so worried about you."

"Yeah, yeah Carol I know I love you too, but would you do me a favor? I must have misplaced my cell phone somewhere. I think I'm going to have to double up on that GINKO shit. With all the crap that's been going on, my memory is getting really interrupted.

THE END

www.ingramcontent.com/pod-product-compliance
Lightning Source LLC
Chambersburg PA
CBHW051511170626
46811CB00002B/755

* 9 7 8 0 6 9 2 2 6 5 0 9 3 *